Trick Shot

**A SPICY
CHRISTMAS
NOVELLA**

By Kayla Grosse

To request permissions, contact the author at

www.kaylagrosse.com

Published by Kayla Grosse

Printed in the United States of America

First US Edition: November 2023

ISBN: 979-8-9870546-2-8 (paperback)

Edited by Swati Hedge

Cover Art by Mel (IG: @mellendraws)

Cover Design by Kayla Grosse

Layout by Nicole Reeves

To all the ho-ho-ho's.
May your jingle balls be merry and bright...
and may this smut satisfy you all through the night.

Author's Note

HAPPY HOLIDAYS!

This is spicy Christmas MMF romance.

This book celebrates love in all shapes and sizes. It contains light bondage, light D/s scenes, light humiliation, light degradation, insertion, and scenes between two men and one woman, including male/male sex. If this is not your cup of tea, please do not read on. As always, take care of yourself. This book is meant to be fun and titillating to get you in the holiday spirit ;)

Now, if you're still here...

Woo-hoo!

Grab a cup of cocoa or a holiday COCKtail, suspend reality for a bit, and cozy up to Leo, Jace, and Riley for a sexy night of Christmas debauchery.

Jace's Holiday COCKtail Recipe:

Ingredients
1 cup sugar
2 sprigs of rosemary (plus more for garnish if desired)
No sugar added cranberry juice not from concentrate
Cranberry lime seltzer water (or flavor of choice)
2oz of Vodka (if desired)
Fresh lime juice (if desired)

For the syrup:
Combine the sugar, rosemary, and 1 cup of water in a small saucepan over medium-high heat. Stir until sugar is dissolved. Remove from heat and allow to cool. Remove the rosemary sprigs and pour the syrup into another small jar.

For the drink:
Grab your favorite cocktail glass and fill it with 1oz of rosemary simple syrup, 2oz of Vodka, 1-2oz of cranberry juice, depending on your taste, and fill to the top with the seltzer. Add a splash of lime juice if you like your drink tart, or more sugar if you like it sweeter. This can be made with or without the Vodka. Add a sprig of rosemary to make it more fun and enjoy!

Trick Shot Unhinged Holiday Playlist

"Let It Snow! "Let It Snow! "Let It Snow!" Frank Sinatra
"Blue Christmas" Elvis Presley
"All I Want for Christmas Is You" Mariah Carey
"White Christmas" Frank Sinatra
"Livin' la Vida Loca" Ricky Martin
"One Margarita (Margarita Song)" by That Chick Angel
"WAP (feat. Megan Thee Stallion)" Cardi B & Megan Thee
Stallion
"Underneath the Tree" Kelly Clarkson
"Freek-A-Leek" Petey Pablo
"S&M Remix" by Rihanna & Britney Spears
"SLUT ME OUT" NLE Choppa
"Here Comes Santa Claus" Elvis Presley
"Santa Baby" Eartha Kitt
"The Christmas Song" Nat King Cole
"The Twelve Days Of Christmas" Bing Crosby & The Andrews
Sisters

CHAPTER ONE

Leo

"Lucas isn't going to take that deal. He won't do anything less than two million."

"We can do as high as one-point-five."

"Two million."

"Come on, Leo. This is a great deal for an NHL player. Tell your brother—"

"Don't pull that on me, Marcus. I'm his agent, and Lucas McKnight isn't just an NHL player—he just got nominated for an Emmy, for God's sake. He'll take two million, or we'll walk."

Marcus sighs loudly on the other end of the line. Not very fucking professional, if you ask me. He's trying to pull his friend card, and it's not going to fucking work.

"The brand doesn't want to spend this much at Christmas time."

"Then this conversation is over. Go get a player that's looking for a bone. Have a great holiday, Marcus." I pretend to hang up, but I know he's not going to say no.

"Wait!"

I smile to myself. "Yes?"

"We'll do two million."

"Great, send over the paperwork to my office, and I'll have him sign. Merry Christmas, Marcus."

After he hangs up without another word, I mentally pat myself on the back. That was too easy. But my brother will be happy, and I'll take that ten percent cut any day of the week.

I'll call it a Christmas bonus. Not that Lucas hasn't given me a hefty one already, but now I can try to relax a bit before things pick up again in the New Year.

I write a text to my identical twin, letting him know it's done. He sends back a stupid confetti GIF as I order a whiskey from the airport bartender. I'm on my way home from New York to Seattle, so I'll be seeing him soon—no need to call, or he'll talk my ear off for an hour. He may be one of the biggest hockey players in the world, and now a TV star, but he's still a loveable idiot who doesn't know when to stop talking. Our mom jokes it's because he came out of the womb after me and thus got the annoying younger sibling gene. I, on the other hand, came out as an "old soul." She used to dress me in little suits and say I'd be a lawyer someday. I may not be a lawyer, but I *am* one of the best sports agents in the business that can negotiate multi-million dollar deals in their sleep.

My phone buzzes, and I look down at the airline notification on my screen. My flight's been delayed due to the weather once already, and now it's happened again. Great. I've never been one for holiday celebrations; there's too much noise and mindless chatter with relatives you only see once a year who just want to talk hockey and ask what celebrities you've met. But Mom wants the whole family home for Christmas dinner tomorrow, as she does every year. So I'll go and put on my best smile for her.

I stop the bartender. "Can you change one of these TVs to the Weather Channel?"

"Sure thing. Though you may find it depressing."

I snicker and take a drink of the top shelf whiskey. Well, as top shelf as this bar in LaGuardia Airport can provide on Christmas Eve.

"Oh god, I hope it doesn't tell me what I think I already know."

My skin prickles pleasantly at the musical sound of the woman's voice. I drag my gaze from the TV toward the source.

She's plump, her cheeks red as if she's run the entire length of the airport, and her mid-length strawberry-blonde hair is frizzy around her round face. She also looks like she's about to cry. Or scream. Or both.

I take a sip of my drink, glad that I'm more Scrooge than Santa during this time of year. Mom will be sad if I don't make it home tonight, but she'll survive. I'll be happy to go home, where my best friend Jace is staying while I'm gone. We'll probably drink too much, fuck each other stupid, then end up in a pile by the fireplace under one of the Christmas trees he forced me to get. All of that sounds significantly better than being on a long flight after waiting in this damn airport for hours. I'm in the mood to celebrate. And kinky sex with Jace is always a good time.

This woman, on the other hand, judging by the tight green pants and red sweatshirt she's wearing, will be devastated not to get where she's going. She watches the weather report with rapt attention, a drip of sweat sliding from her temple as her face contorts in despair.

"I knew I should have left yesterday." She groans. "Stupid Chad!"

I bite the inside of my cheek to keep from laughing. "Chads are usually stupid."

The woman turns at my comment, her green eyes widening when she sees me. I know that look. It's the one I get multiple times a day. The one the bartender gave me when I first sat down. The downside of having a twin brother who's famous as fuck is that people always think I'm him. It's not their fault, either. If you don't personally know me and Lucas, it's hard to tell us apart. I even walked a red carpet last year for him when he'd partied a little too hard the night before. We've been impersonating each other since we knew we could get away with it. The only people it doesn't work on are our mom and Jace. Even our dad can be fooled.

"Um, you're—you're, um," she fumbles.

I raise my hands up, not letting her finish the sentence. "Guilty as charged."

Her mouth drops open. I can tell by the glint in her eye she's a fan—maybe even one of the obsessive ones. I don't have the heart to tell her I'm not him. Especially considering she's most likely going to be stuck in this airport or on her way back to where she came from shortly.

"Wow. That's, uh. Wow," she says.

Then she surprises me. She turns and flags the bartender down, ordering a dry martini with an extra olive. Her neck flushes and she mutters something about just her luck wearing a stupid outfit today. I think I hear "the hottest man alive" at some point, which makes me smile. She's cute, and I like the way her skin is starting to match the color of her hair. When she gets her drink, she downs it, then orders another one, muttering about Chad again.

"What did Chad do to you, Shortcake?"

Her skin stains impossibly red as her eyes lock with mine. They're pretty, like the color of pine trees against white snow.

"Shortcake?" she huffs. "I'm tall."

She's right; she is tall, by the looks of her long, shapely legs. However, I'm 6'2". But that's not why I called her 'shortcake.' "Your skin," I grin, "reminds me of my favorite dessert. Strawberry Shortcake."

Her mouth drops open, shocked at my bold flirting. I go to backtrack, to say sorry for being so forward, but then she stops me with that musical voice of hers.

"Do I get to call you a nickname, then?"

I raise an eyebrow at her. Oh, so she likes to play, too. "If you'd like."

She grabs the new martini and takes the olive from the glass. She closes her pouty lips around it and sucks it into her mouth before chewing slowly. Suddenly, my Armani pants are tight, and I find myself shifting on the barstool.

"How about," she hums around the next olive, "Beefcake?"

I let out a bark of laughter. "That's original."

The flush that was starting to leave her skin comes back in full force. "I never said I was good at giving nicknames."

"So what are you good at?" I ask.

She taps her white painted nails on the bar countertop. "Nothing, if you ask Chad."

"You're right. Chad *is* stupid."

A smile curls at her glossy lips before she holds out her hand. "I'm Riley."

I put my drink down and engulf her hand with mine. Her touch is clammy, but I like the feeling of her cool rings against my palm.

"Nice to meet you, Riley." I don't bother saying my name. We've already established that she thinks I'm Lucas.

Her smile turns shy as she pulls her hand back. "I'm sorry for my reaction earlier. It's not every day you see one of America's hottest bachelors at an airport bar on Christmas Eve. I'd think, if anything, you'd have a private jet or be on a tropical island somewhere, avoiding snow! I mean, I guess you're a hockey player so you probably like snow. But again, maybe you need a break. I know I'd probably need a break from the schedule you have, and a beach sounds lovely this time of year."

My gaze tracks to her lips as she rambles. They're plush yet delicate-looking, just like the rest of her body. It's then I notice the sweater has a deep V-neck, and there's a snowflake pendant resting between the voluptuous valley of her tits. Shit, maybe I should just call it a night and head back to my place. Now I'm horny as hell, and while Jace may not have breasts, he's soft in all the places I like. For a split second, I think of this beautiful woman sandwiched between me and my best friend—and now my cock is definitely hard.

"Oh my god, I'm rambling and embarrassing you. My sister Stevie makes fun of me for going on tangents when I get nervous. And well, you're you, and I'm...well, me!"

I flick my ice-blue eyes to hers and will myself to remain calm. At least she's mistaken the color in my cheeks from embarrassment, instead of me staring at her boobs.

"You don't have to be nervous, Shortcake. I'm just a guy."

That makes her bark out a laugh. "You're anything but that."

"So people think." I shrug. "Though behind everything, I'm just that. A man."

She hums. "I suppose that's true. So tell me, what are you doing here on Christmas Eve, Just a Guy?"

I glance at my phone and see there's no updates on my flight yet. "Same as you, I suppose. Though I can't blame Chad for any of this."

She downs the rest of her martini and huffs. "You should. Chad ruins everything."

I flag the bartender and tell him to get us both another round. She smiles gratefully and tries to relax on the stool, but they don't have much surface area. These things were not created for comfort. I notice a pair of chairs in the corner just vacated, and I find myself standing.

"Care to join me?"

Riley looks to the corner, her face that of disbelief. "Me?"

"Yeah, Shortcake. You." To be honest, I don't know why I asked, either. But she's sexy and sweet. And I do need to wait until my flight is actually canceled before I leave the airport, or my mom and Lucas will know I bailed.

She takes the fresh martini and grabs the handle of her carry-on, moving to the corner in almost a state of shock. I quietly tell the bartender to put her drinks on my tab, then follow her. There are some Christmas lights and holly above the chairs. The multi-colored lights cast a festive glow on her fair skin and strawberry hair. She almost looks like she was pulled from a snow globe.

She sits and settles in, sighing as she takes another sip of the drink. Once I've done the same, she stares at me.

"Sorry again for my rambling," she says. "I thought it would've scared you off."

"Takes a lot more than that to scare me."

"Oh god, I hope you don't think I'm one of your stalkers, or something."

"Are you?"

She huffs a small laugh. "No, no. My sister is a huge fan of yours. She'll hate me forever when I tell her I met the star Forward of the Seattle Stormbreakers."

"You're saying you're not a fan of me, then? Or you're just not a stalker."

That pretty flush returns. "Of course I'm a fan. Who isn't?"

"Lots of people. Especially Canadians."

She snorts. "I'm not going to lie, I don't really know much about hockey. I watched you on that Netflix show. It was good."

I nod, feeling slightly uncomfortable she's giving Lucas compliments and not me. But it's also nice to not be 'Lucas McKnight's brother' for a moment. If I tell her the truth, she'll probably give me 'the Look.' The one that says, "*Oh! You're the brother that 'could have been' one of the great Hockey players if you didn't have a career ending injury, and now you're just his agent."* Jace will call me an idiot when I tell him about all this, but I think he also understands why I don't correct people. It's just easier to go with it.

I can't stop the small smile that tugs at my lips when thinking of Jace. He's a godsend, and always has been. I met him in college thirteen years ago in a dive bar right after I was told I'd never be able to play hockey at a professional level because of a knee injury I sustained during a fucking scrimmage gone wrong. And while our relationship didn't cross over from friends to friends with benefits until a few years ago, things have always been easy with him. He's never expected anything outside of what I can offer. He understands that while I'm out as pansexual, with the industry we work in and who I'm related to, it's hard to have relationships—especially unique ones.

That's also just part of it. On top of loving whoever the fuck I want to, I've never been one for the traditional when it comes to relationships and sex. Monogamy just never sounded appealing. Thankfully, Jace feels the same. Though recently we've both been so busy with our clients that we've been fucking each other more often. Just last night, he joked how I need to meet more people, or his dick is going to fall off from my sexual appetite. So, as I look at Riley's soft body and perfect tits, my dick recalls the way she flirted with that olive. This could be an opportunity to taste a different flavor for tonight. Maybe she'd be open to Jace and me, together.

I can see it now: Those pretty red lips of hers around my cock while Jace rails her from behind.

Blood rushes back to my crotch, and I shift in my chair. I don't know what it is about this woman that has me so tightly wound. We just met, and while I know she's Lucas's fan, I don't know if she's the one-night stand type of woman. Or what type of woman she is, at all. Just because she's flirting doesn't mean she'd be open to a three-way on Christmas Eve. For now, I decide to get to know this alluring stranger better while I can.

"Tell me about Chad," I say. Immediately, her demeanor changes. Her shoulders tense and her forehead creases.

"I don't want to ruin your Christmas."

My hand seems to move on its own as I place it on her shoulder and squeeze. Her doe eyes look into mine, which doesn't help my previous thoughts.

"I'm in the airport on Christmas Eve getting tipsy on subpar whiskey. You're not ruining my Christmas," I assure her. I remove my hand from her shoulder and immediately miss the warm feel of her soft sweater beneath my palm.

She sighs. "He's my ex. My ex that I work with. We broke up over a year ago, but he loves to find ways to screw with my life. Even though he's the one who cheated on me."

My jaw clenches, feeling bad for this person I hardly know. "How so?"

She motions to her outfit. "He made me wear this for a last-minute pitch, which went way over because he would not stop talking out of his own ass. That's why I was late getting to the airport and I wasn't able to change. I thought I was going to miss my flight until they delayed it again."

"Something tells me that's not why you're upset at him."

She takes another drink. "You're observant."

"Helps with my job." She doesn't know I'm not referring to hockey, but it works all the same.

"I suppose that's true." She plays with one of the sparkly rings around her finger. "He insisted on driving me to the airport. Anyway, let's just say that he's an asshole, and I should've taken a cab."

I study her as she shifts the ring she's been twisting into its original position and takes a deep breath. I shouldn't have asked about Chad. I have no business involving myself in her life. But right now, that's all I care about. I want to know everything about this asshole so I can go pummel his face in.

"What do you do that had you doing a presentation on Christmas Eve?" I ask, wanting to know more.

She throws up her hands. "That's the thing. This meeting could have waited until the New Year. I work at a digital ad agency, and one of our clients is a friend of Chad's. For some reason, this meeting had to happen this afternoon. And I had to be festive! Chad told me he was doing the same, but of course, he looked like he was ready to go to a five-star dinner on the Upper East Side while I look like a Christmas card. He did it on purpose. He likes to demean me as punishment for breaking up with him."

I clench my fist around my glass. "There aren't any other agencies you could work at in the city?" I start to think of friends I know in the industry, ones who could possibly help her out.

"I refuse to quit because a man is having a temper tantrum over something he caused." She makes a fair point there. "And this agency was a dream of mine to work at since I was in college. It's the sole reason I moved from Seattle to New York."

Now her sister's obsession with Lucas makes even more sense. Everyone in Seattle knows who my brother is.

I nod. "Well, if you ever decide you want a change, I know a lot of people who work in your field. If you need a referral, I'd be more than willing."

Surprise colors her features. "You don't even know me. Maybe I *am* a stalker."

I chuckle. "I'll admit, I thought you could be at first, with the rambling and how you reacted when you saw me. But now, I think I like you, Riley. I'm good at reading people. Plus, you're a follow Seattleite, so I have to like you." I wink at the last part.

She blushes. "Are you sure you're a hockey player?"

My heart stops for a second. "Why?"

"I grew up around a lot of them. You're...different."

"You mean I have all my teeth."

She laughs, a small snort escaping. "Exactly."

"I guess I'll take that as a compliment, then." My phone pings, and I see it's from Jace. He's asking if my flight is canceled. They're talking about shutting down the subways, which means it must be getting rough out there. Just as I'm about to tell him it's still delayed, I get a message from the airline saying my flight is canceled. By the sound that comes out of Riley, we must be on the same plane.

"Damn it. Stevie is going to be so disappointed," she says, her voice tight with emotion and eyes a bit glassy.

"I'm sorry."

She shrugs. "Nothing for you to be sorry about. You didn't cancel the flight." A few more choice words about Chad leave her mouth before she stands. "I better get to the train before the whole airport gets there. It was nice meeting you."

The idea of her leaving has my stomach flipping over and me standing up with her. It stuns me briefly, because I'm usually not this way with a person I just met. When my phone pings again, I force the feeling away and see Jace's message that he's already halfway to the airport. He assumed this was going to happen, and started the trek before the roads got worse. I feel a surge of gratitude at his ability to plan ahead.

"Where's your place?" I ask Riley.

Her watery eyes are now replaced with that flirty glint from earlier. The one she had while sucking on that olive.

"You want to come home with me, Beefcake?" she asks.

My cock stirs again, and I smirk just enough so she can see the lone dimple on my right cheek. "I won't say no, but I was going to offer you a ride home."

Her skin goes pink as she wrings her hands together. "Oh...No, no. That's okay, I can make it home."

Excitement sparks in my veins at the disappointment in her tone. She's embarrassed because she thinks I wasn't thinking about fucking her. Which means that she *was* thinking about fucking me. This woman is a surprise. An unexpected gift in an overcrowded airport, and I want to unwrap her—in more ways than one.

Without another word, she makes her way to the bar and I quickly follow.

"I took care of it," I tell her. When the bartender hands me my card, I sign the slip of paper, adding a generous tip.

"You didn't have to do that."

"It's my pleasure."

When our eyes connect, the busy airport fades into the background, a spark of energy passing between us. The same one I felt when I first heard her musical voice. At the time, I didn't think much of it—now I want to revel in it.

She takes her lower lip between her teeth and gently bites down. When her eyes drop to my mouth, I can't help but reach out and pull her lip from its grasp. I rub my thumb over the indented skin and feel her short breaths heat my hand. When I move my finger down the curve of her rounded jaw, she shivers, and the image in my mind becomes clearer.

If Riley comes home with me tonight, Jace and I will treat her like a queen. We'll feed her a delicious meal before stripping her bare and eating her out like a five-star dessert. Maybe she'll even let Jace tie her up in his favorite red rope. Goddamn, she'll make a beautiful sight under our tree, decorated in ornaments of all kinds.

But even more than that, there's something about Riley that makes me want to know her more than just biblically. I want to hear what Chad said to her on the way to the airport. I want to know what she likes to eat, and I want to hear her laugh at one of Jace's stupid dad jokes. It sounds dumb, considering we met thirty minutes ago, but there's a nagging feeling in my gut that's telling me I can't let Riley walk away.

"Riley—"

"Lucas—"

We speak at the same time and both laugh from it. I lower my hand to take hers, ignoring the pesky fact that she still thinks I'm Lucas.

"You go first," she urges me.

"I asked where you lived, but what I really should have asked is: Would you like to spend Christmas Eve with me?"

Her face lights up, but I notice the trepidation mixed in as well.

I squeeze her hand. "There aren't any expectations, of course. I have a spare room, and my penthouse is decorated to the nines. It won't make up for missing Christmas morning with your family, but my friend Jace can make us breakfast when we wake up. I promise, he's a good guy. Though he does like to bite." I wink.

She chuckles, probably trying to determine if my words are true.

"I have to admit," she says, "this is not how I expected tonight to go."

I brush my thumb over her knuckle. "That a good or a bad thing?"

Her gaze locks with mine, eyes sparkling. "I think it's a good thing."

"So you'll come home with me?"

She grins cheekily. "Do you bite?"

I lean forward and put my lips to her ear. "Only if you ask me to, Shortcake."

Her breath hitches, and I notice the way her thighs squeeze together. She's turned on, and nothing's even happened yet. Oh yeah, this woman was sent to me by fate—or maybe by Santa.

My phone pings, and I tug on her hand. "Come on. That's probably Jace."

CHAPTER TWO

Riley

JIMINY CHRISTMAS! I CAN'T believe this is happening to me. ME.

Boring, old Riley. Silly, old, dependable Riley. Stick up her ass, won't go out after eight in the evening on a weeknight, Riley is now on her way to a complete stranger's house on Christmas Eve.

Is he really a stranger, though?

I mean, he is, but he's famous. If he kills me, he'll never get away with it. I know that's stupid logic, but hell—this is a once-in-a-lifetime chance. I'm willing to throw caution to the wind on this occasion. Call it a Christmas present to myself.

With a bit of newfound confidence, Lucas and I walk through the crowded airport while I shoot a quick text to my mom that my flight is canceled. I'll have to send a more detailed message to my sister in the car. Stevie will be upset I'm not there for our Christmas morning traditions, but when I tell her who I was with, she'll probably forgive me. Or never talk to me again because she'll wish it was her.

Lucas presses one of his large hands into my lower back, and I shiver. Jesus, this man is a snack. To see him in pictures and TV is one thing—but in person? He's like a statue, chiseled and blessed by God himself. It's sort of hard to look him in the eye because he's almost too perfect. Not only is he tall and built, but his textured midnight black hair just screams for me to run my hands through it. And those blue eyes!

"Everything okay?" he asks.

I bob my head, unable to form words at the moment. I'm still trying to process what I'm doing and who I'm probably going to be doing later. This kind of thing just doesn't happen to normal everyday people. You don't just meet a celebrity in the airport like this. He even gave me a nickname. My belly flip flops when I think of the way he calls me 'Shortcake.'

"You sure?" he asks again.

"Everything's good," I finally manage to say.

"Good." He smiles, and my body heats up. That damn one dimple is a panty-dropper in itself.

When we reach the doors, I stop to put on my red peacoat and candy cane scarf. It makes me want to gag just looking at it.

"You really know how to take festive to a new level, don't you?" Lucas chuckles.

"This is all Chad's fault, remember?"

He snorts, putting on his fleece-lined bomber jacket. I swallow the lump in my throat at the sight of him. While I look like Mrs. Claus, he looks like a model fresh off a winter runway. I bite my lower lip, and his eyes track the movement. He's been doing that a lot, which makes me believe he does want to kiss me. Well, he implied he would be open to more than kissing if I wanted. But there's also the matter of this Jace guy. Is he a roommate? And why did I get the feeling Jace would really bite me if I asked him to? That was a joke. It had to have been. Right?

My emotions bloom on my cheeks, sweat gathering at the base of my neck. If I don't walk outside right now, I'm going to overheat.

"Is your friend waiting for us?" I ask, trying to keep my voice free of its lust-induced strain.

We move off to the side of the doors to let others walk out as Lucas taps furiously on his phone. There's a moment where he looks upset, but then he quickly replaces it with a mask of calm and collectedness. I really hope he doesn't have a girlfriend. The media say he's a bachelor, but there's got to be a ton of women lining up to sleep with him. Not just puck bunnies, but actresses and models too. My self-esteem crashes, which doesn't take much right now after Chad took a big bite out of me earlier.

I don't know why I let that bastard get to me. His breath smells, and he's the biggest mama's boy I've ever met. But he was my boyfriend for two years, and I can't help but feel like his opinion of me still matters. And he just loves to put me down. My hair, my clothes, my body, my work—you name it. He always has something to say about all of it.

"Jace is pulling up." Lucas gives me another smile, his eyes dropping to blatantly check me out. When they return to my face, there's a twinkle in his eye that tells me he's thinking something devious. It's then I decide I need to knock off my horrendous inner dialogue. I've been working on self-love for the past year, and it's time I put all those self-help books and morning mirror mantras to good use. I am enough. I'm fucking hot and beautiful. Men love my softness, and so do I. The reality that Lucas could have anyone and he chose me? I should take that as a huge self-esteem boost, not the other way around.

Screw Chad and his stupid words.

I'm getting laid by a sexy-as-fuck hockey player tonight. My mind is made up.

CHAPTER THREE

Jace

THE COOL TONES OF Frank Sinatra singing "White Christmas" over the radio are very on the nose as I wait for the light to turn green. I tighten my gloved hand around the steering wheel of my Jeep Renegade, while absentmindedly scratching my beard with the other. I press my lips together, picturing said hands throttling Leo's perfectly pretty throat for the text message I just received.

My best friend is several things. He's smart, funny, loyal—he's also one of the kindest people I've ever known (if you don't get on his bad side). Not to mention one of the most adventurous sexual partners I've ever had. But one thing he's never been good at is admitting when he's fucked up.

I listen to the text he sent over the car speaker again, and I have to stop myself from rolling my eyes. He's bringing a woman from the airport home to spend Christmas Eve with us, one I assume he wants to share his bed with, but the kicker is—she thinks he's Lucas. He's pretended to be Lucas on other occasions, and I've always thought it was stupid. If he were to get caught, there'd be a media shitstorm. I don't know the whole story of why she thinks he's Lucas, or why he couldn't just say he's his twin, but his text begged me to keep my mouth shut. And I'm nothing if not a good boy, at least when I want to be.

When I pull up to Terminal 1, there aren't many cars out besides a bunch of cabs, yet I'm glad I came when I did. It's probably going to take us a while to get home, and with how bad the roads are, I couldn't let Leo sit at the airport on Christmas Eve. He wouldn't have cared, but I do. While I don't celebrate Christmas with my family in Honolulu anymore, and haven't since I came out to them as bisexual years ago, I have my friends and Leo. I've grown to find peace and so much love in celebrating holidays with my found family. I also have plenty of new fun traditions with said friends. Including one of my favorites: sex under the Christmas tree. Which Leo and I enjoyed alone together last night, since he was supposed to be on a plane to Seattle tonight.

Now with a smirk on my face, I put the car into park and send Leo a text to let him know I'm here. Less than a minute later, I see his tall form walking out along with a vision in red. She looks like a walking candy cane, her red peacoat hugging her ample form as snow clings to her coppery-blonde hair. It's amusing to me that Mr. Scrooge happened to attract someone who looks like she enjoys Christmas way more than he ever has in his life.

As I pop the trunk, I overhear Leo insist on helping her with her bag. Her voice is lyrical as she thanks him, and the hair on my arms stands on end. I enjoy sleeping with women, and often, Leo and I share, but it's been several months since I've felt anything other than the hard planes of my friend's body. It would be nice to wrap myself in something that smells sweet. I bet she tastes sweet, too. When I catch Leo's eyes in the rearview mirror, the look he's giving me says he's thinking the exact same thing.

He slams the trunk of my jeep closed, and I track Ms. Candy Cane as she makes her way to the front door. When she climbs in, I'm hit with the smell of her perfume, floral and honeyed. My cock wakes up, and I send a little Christmas prayer to whoever is listening that this mystery woman will be willing to let both Leo—or should I say Lucas—and myself have some fun with her tonight.

"Hi, I'm Riley." She smiles, her green eyes dark in the low light. "Thanks for picking us up."

My cock grows harder, and her words weren't even sexual. Leo has always had good taste in people, but Riley is an absolute dream. I've already started to imagine what those curves look like under her coat, and what her hair will feel like wrapped around my fist or brushing against my hips as she wraps those lips around my cock. It's only when Leo clears his throat that I realize I'm staring. I try to cover it up with a warm smile.

"Hi, Riley, I'm Jace." Miraculously, my voice comes out steady. "And it's no problem at all."

She blushes for whatever reason, and my eyes move to look at Leo's via the rearview mirror. He's buckling his seatbelt, but his gaze is glued to my face. We speak without words like we have for years now, and I can't help but give him a nod in approval. His lustful stare tells me everything I need to know. That he wants Riley to not just be his tonight, but ours.

"You good, *Lucas*?" I make sure to emphasize his "name." The warmth in his blue eyes fades, and he narrows them at me. I put away my desire to flip him off, turning my attention back to the angel in my front seat.

"You buckled in, beautiful?"

She ducks her head at the praise and rubs her hands together, which prompts me to turn up the heat. I've always run hot, so my car is never warm enough in the winter according to Leo.

"I'm in," she voices.

I meet Leo's eyes again. He looks like a fox in a henhouse, and I can't help but feel like this night is going to be one we never forget.

I just hope Riley knows what she's in for—and Leo, aka Lucas, knows what he's doing.

CHAPTER FOUR

Leo

THE DRIVE HOME WAS slow. The roads were shit, and I'm shocked Jace even made it to the airport. Had I really known how terrible it was, I would have insisted he stay home and I get a hotel for the night—granted, they're probably all booked out.

The ride was nice, though. I've gotten so used to only seeing Jace, Lucas, and my other male clients in the last few months that I've forgotten what it's like to have a woman's energy in my sphere. And despite the snowstorm—and that she isn't flying home tonight—Riley's spirits are high. It helps that she and Jace hit it off. The entire drive, they were comparing their terrible taste in music (like Ricky Martin's "Livin' La Vida Loca") and their love for tacos. I didn't chime in much, instead enjoying the sound of my best friend's laugh and getting to know the strawberry-blonde beauty next to him. I also won't lie that I've been imagining how to convince Riley to let both Jace and me worship her. I saw the look in his eye earlier, and I know he wants it just as much as I do.

"Welcome to my home," I say to her, pushing open the door to my penthouse.

Riley's eyes are bright with wonder as she takes in the large open space decked out in holiday decor. Her gaze has been like that since the moment we stepped into the ornate lobby where our doorman Arnold greeted us and soft music played. She must make a good living doing what she does, but I know where I live is ostentatious and ridiculous. Even I sometimes can't believe it, and I never take it for granted.

"Wow," she gasps as the lights come on, "This is...this is wow. I always see these places on social media, but I never thought I'd ever be inside one."

Without prompting, she makes her way to the wall of expansive floor-to-ceiling windows with a panoramic view of the city and Central Park.

"I can't wait to see this in the morning," she adds. "I bet the snow will make it look like a Christmas movie."

"I can confirm, it does look like that," Jace says, removing his coat before walking to my wet bar. "Who wants a drink? I make a mean festive cocktail."

I think about the whiskey I drank at the airport, but decide to hell with it. I'm not feeling drunk or even tipsy anymore. "I'll take one."

"Sure," Riley says. "Though make mine half strength, or I'll be asleep before you put the milk and cookies out for Santa Claus."

Jace grins. "That reminds me of a joke."

I cringe. "Oh boy. Jace, please don't scare her away before she even takes her coat off."

A smile decorates Riley's lips. "I want to hear it."

Jace rubs his hands together in glee. "Why did Santa divorce Mrs. Claus?"

"I don't know, why did she?" Riley asks.

"He was obsessed with getting the cookie."

Riley lets out a cute snort-giggle that gets us both chuckling with her. "That was really silly," she says.

"Plenty more where that came from," Jace replies, grabbing a shaker.

"One is good, J," I remind him. "There are only so many dirty Santa jokes a person can take. I would know."

Jace smirks at me. "You know you like it. You just laughed!"

I shake my head, then turn my attention to Riley, taking her discarded scarf and coat from her. "Make yourself comfortable, Shortcake."

"Shortcake?" Jace asks with curiosity. "But she's tall."

Riley laughs. "That's what I said!"

"Her hair *is* strawberry-blonde. But it's because she blushes like—"

Riley slaps her hand over my mouth, and Jace's eyebrows shoot up. I do the only mature thing and lick her palm, grinning like an idiot when she pulls her hand away.

"You just licked me!"

I lean down so I'm level with her ear. I know Jace can hear me, but I don't care. "That was just a taste test."

Her cheeks stain as Jace walks over with our cocktails, some cranberry concoction he's been obsessed with. He hands Riley the drink, then his devious hazel eyes flash to me.

"I get the Shortcake nickname now. And I just so happen to like that treat, too."

Riley's mouth opens softly as she clutches the glass. I notice the way her breasts rise and fall with the change in her breathing. I wonder if her nipples are hard underneath her clothing. I'd bet a million dollars they are.

After a moment, she closes her mouth, then darts toward the black leather couch in the living room and out of our reach. I take my drink from Jace, and he pats me on the shoulder, as if to say, *Give it time.* Then he walks off to join Riley, taking a seat in the chair across from her. He crosses one of his legs, resting an ankle on his knee like he does and relaxes back.

Normally, Jace would be dressed in his usual jeans and button-up, but he must've been getting ready to chill when he jumped in his car. His medium-length brown hair is mussed from running his hands through it, and he's wearing a pair of dark green sweatpants and a gray long-sleeved Henley that shows off the outline of the tree trunks he calls arms. He looks good. Granted, I always think he's attractive, no matter what he's wearing.

A little moan from Riley breaks my focus on Jace.

"Wow, that's really good," she says, savoring her drink. "Is there rosemary in here?"

Jace's eyes shine at her approval. "There is. It's a simple syrup I make."

"Are you a bartender?"

He exhales a laugh. "Once upon a time, when I was young and trying to make ends meet. Now it's just a fun thing I like to do to unwind. I use Leo as a taste tester."

My back stiffens at the sound of my name.

"Who's Leo?"

Jace doesn't look at me, but his jaw ticks. "He's Lucas's identical twin."

"Oh that's right! I totally forgot you have a twin, Lucas. That must be so cool!" More relaxed now, Riley pats the spot next to her on the couch. I try to breathe and stay calm as I take a seat.

I can feel Jace's judgmental gaze burning me as I choose my next words carefully. "It can be. Though I know it's difficult for Leo sometimes. I can overshadow him just because of who I am."

The words are like acid on my tongue. Even though it's my truth, it's one I don't admit often. And I'm not even admitting it as me. I should just stop the ruse now and tell Riley the truth. She seems like an understanding person, and she'd probably be mad but get over it. Yet I can't bring myself to say anything.

Her warm hand rests on my thigh. "I'm sure he doesn't really feel that way. He's your brother."

"Yeah, Lucas. He's your brother," Jace chides.

I stare down my supposed best friend. He's not making this easy on me. And despite it being my fault that this is happening right now, I can't help but be annoyed at him. He knows how I feel sometimes, but he also can't completely get it. I live a privileged life, and my brother is everything to me. But as

I've made known, it can be hard to live in a world that only recognizes me as Lucas or the brother that *"could have made it to the NHL,"* that *"could have been great."*

I have a lot of accomplishments as an agent in the industry, including my own goddamn agency with high-profile clients, but it's often overlooked because of those reasons. And while I don't necessarily need the recognition, it would be nice to be just Leo for once. A man who made himself into something after losing what he thought was everything.

Riley's eyes bounce between Jace and me. I know she can feel the tension. So I lean my body in closer to her, erasing the anger and sadness that's threatening to spill out, and bring a lock of her wavy hair into my fingers. "Is this your natural color?"

Her body eases and I ignore Jace, who's most likely rolling his eyes. Maybe I'll spank him for it later. "It's not. I have light brown hair. I've been experimenting with different colors since Chad and I broke up last year. First I went blonde, then I wanted to look like Rachel McAdams in her *Notebook* era."

"It suits you, Shortcake." That blush returns, and I tug on the lock of hair a bit. She captures her lower lip between her teeth again. This time, when my cock stirs, I don't try to quell it.

"Thanks, Beefcake." She smirks.

Jace expels a bawdy laugh. "Now that's a great nickname."

Riley beams at him. "Why, thank you. At least you appreciate it, Jace."

I release her hair and give her a dimpled smile. "It's growing on me."

Riley looks happy at that as she takes a swig of her cocktail, settling back so her thigh now touches mine. The warmth is searing, and I find myself melting into her as much as I can in this position.

"So tell me, how did you two meet?" she asks.

Jace leans forward so his arms are on his knees, looking at me expectantly. If I tell the truth, it will give me away. So again, I lie. "He works with Leo."

"And what do you do, Jace?" she asks.

"I'm a senior agent at Leo's agency. I rep mostly hockey players, but a few figure skaters as well."

I swallow the lump in my throat, grateful that's all he's saying.

"That's really cool!" Her smile is contagious as she continues, "So you live here with Lucas, or?"

Again, Riley looks between us. The tone in her voice gives away what she's really asking. Not everyone catches on to that Jace and I have a different type of relationship, but Riley's smart. Between my comments at the airport and the casual way Jace lounges in my home, I'm sure it seems odd. I also have never tried to hide the way I look at him or he at me.

I lean forward, taking the drink from Riley's hand. I place both our glasses on the side table next to her. She stops breathing at my nearness, and goosebumps fan out across my skin from being so close to her.

"Would it bother you if I said that Jace and I are together?"

My hand caresses the skin near the V of her neckline before I finger the snowflake pendant between her breasts. The room goes quiet, and I'm pretty sure Jace has stopped breathing as well. I don't think he expected me to dive right in, but we're wasting time just talking.

"You're together, together?" she asks quietly.

Riley looks to Jace, and he smiles lazily at her. "Depends on what you think that means, Shortcake," he says. Her nickname sounds nice on his lips, and the desire to hear him call her that as she sucks his massive cock has my own now aching against the zipper of my pants.

I take Riley's chin between my thumb and pointer finger, directing her focus back to me. "In most senses of the word, yes," I say. "Though we've both agreed that 'boyfriend' doesn't exactly fit what he is to me or I am to him. We're also non-traditional."

She mulls over what I've just told her.

"We don't have labels," I continue. "He's my best friend, someone I love and care for."

"You're confusing her, Beefcake." Jace laughs quietly.

The corners of my lips turn up at the endearment. "What I'm trying to say is that we're both commitment-phobes with insane schedules who enjoy and crave each other's company. We both love sex, we're both queer, and we both enjoy having the freedom to fuck other people, both separately and together. So no, we aren't together in the traditional sense, but we are at the same time."

Jace moves off the chair and perches on the arm of the couch next to her. "I'm not sure that helped. Did that help, Riley?" he asks.

She plays with her ring again, a blush rising along the crest of her tits. She's not looking at Jace or me, and after a minute, I start to get concerned that maybe I misread her. I eye Jace, but he doesn't seem concerned. Just calm and patient, like always.

Eventually, she looks up, but I can't read her. "Can I use your restroom?" she asks me.

Disappointment wells in my stomach. "Of course you can."

"I'll show you where it is," Jace offers.

Then I watch them walk away with a pang in my chest.

CHAPTER FIVE

Riley

I CLOSE THE DOOR of the lavish bathroom and let out a long breath. I can't believe I was right: Jace would totally bite me if I asked him to.

Placing my hands on the black marble sink, I stare at myself in the mirror. My skin is flushed from all the alcohol I've consumed and the hormones coursing through my body. Being close to Lucas, having him touch my skin—it makes my insides light up. I've heard the saying that sometimes you meet people you're just meant to meet, and I feel that with him. There's this pull between us, and I want to explore it.

Then there's Jace. He's a big guy, rounder in the middle, with broad shoulders and a disarming smile. His skin is a warm brown and his shaggy hair and well-trimmed beard does things to me. When he picked us up from the airport, I couldn't help my blush. He has a similar energy to Lucas with his flirtatious ways, but he's also extremely kind and funny. From our talk in the car, I know we have similar interests. My gaze turns to the door where he stood only a minute before.

Could I be with two men at once? I mean, that's what they were implying, right?

"Think, Riley," I tell my reflection.

These men clearly know what they're doing. They said this is something they've done before. They also obviously have something strong between them, it was evident to me the moment we walked in the penthouse and Jace so casually walked around Lucas's space, making drinks and acting like this was his home, too. At first I thought they were just good friends, but I caught the way they intensely gazed at each other when they didn't know I was looking.

In the mirror, my green eyes stare back at me. This is a once-in-a-lifetime experience. I could take it, have an amazing night with these two men, then go on my merry way tomorrow. Or I could go out there, make new friends, then fall asleep and leave in the morning without a single orgasm and the thought of *What if I had?*

"Have some fun, Riley," I tell myself. "For once in your life, do something wild and free."

I smooth my hands over my outfit and think of how I haven't shaved in a week, and I'm positive I'm wearing my least attractive pair of granny panties with a bra that needs to be washed. I mean, I wasn't planning on having sex tonight, until Lucas invited me here. And I for sure wasn't planning on having sex with two men. On Christmas Eve, no less!

Knock, knock, knock.

"Are you okay, Riley?" Lucas asks from the other side of the door.

I pause and remember what I told myself in the airport when I decided to come with Lucas in the first place. I came here to have a fun night, and I wasn't thinking about my prickly legs when I made that decision.

"Shortcake?" he probes, his voice slightly worried now.

I take one last look in the mirror and awkwardly give myself a thumbs up. I'm such a dork. Why did this man bring me home again? No! Nope. Not going there. With a soothing breath, I swing the door open. Lucas is leaning on the door frame, his dark hair mussed and forehead creased. He's changed from his fancy suit and now wears a similar outfit to Jace: gray sweatpants and a charcoal long-sleeved shirt that clings to his muscular form.

"My legs aren't shaved," I blurt out.

Lucas purses his lips as he tries to stop himself from laughing. "Is that why you ran in here?" He starts to back me up, prowling toward me like a lion on the hunt.

"Not really, but that's all I can think about at the moment," I tell him.

That laugh that was on the surface bubbles out of him as he pins me to the glass shower door. The hard planes of his body press into my softness, and I hold back a moan.

He tucks a piece of my hair behind my ear. "And what else are you worried about?"

"I'm wearing granny panties." I swallow. "The kind that sucks all your rolls in. It's not cute."

He lets out an airy sound, running his nose up my cheek and tracing the shell of my ear. I shiver at the sensitive area being teased.

"You don't have to worry about any of that," he says. "I don't care about hair on your legs or what kind of underwear you have on. But I care about you, and I care about your comfort. So tell me, how can I make it better?"

I take in a choppy breath as he gently bites my earlobe. Jesus, this man is goooood.

"My b-bag." I shudder as he kisses my neck. "I have a razor. A-and some cuter underwear."

He sucks on my pulse point, and my knees weaken. Thank goodness he's holding me up, or I'd be a puddle on the floor right now.

"I have a new razor in here you can use. As for the underwear, I plan on you being naked all night. No need for them." His eyes level with mine, our noses now touching. "That is, if you want to get naked with me, Riley?"

He's serious in his question. There's no playfulness there. His demeanor tells me he'll let me leave and walk out into the snowstorm if I say this isn't what I want.

"And Jace, too?" I ask, my voice husky.

Lucas's face lights up, his pupils dilating slightly. "Jace is cooking us a little Christmas Eve feast. He'll join us after we eat if that's what you want."

My throat closes up at their thoughtfulness. It was clear I freaked out when I asked to use the bathroom, and they'd taken notice. But Lucas just proved why I felt safe enough to come home with him after we'd just met. And if I'm not careful, I'll fall for this man. Which is dangerous because he doesn't do relationships. It's a quick and sobering reminder that tonight is it, and I'm going to take full advantage—granny panties be damned.

"I think I'd like that," I finally say.

Lucas releases his beautiful one-dimpled smile on me. "Really?"

I nod. "I've never been with two men at once, so forgive me if I'm awkward. I still can't believe you're both offering. I feel like I'm in some pornographic fever dream."

"Are you kidding, Riley? I can't believe I found a woman like you in an airport sports bar on Christmas Eve. Call this Scrooge converted, because Christmas miracles do exist."

My cheeks burn. "You probably could have found better, but I'm glad it was me nonetheless."

Lucas's jaw clenches. "You're perfect, and don't let boys like Chad ever tell you otherwise."

I purse my lips. "You don't even know me that well."

He brushes an errant strand of hair from my cheek. "I've met a lot of people in my life, Riley. Too many of them are fake assholes who take whatever they want, then leave you to pick up the pieces. You're not one of those people. I don't need to know your life story to make that call."

"Again, I have to ask, are you sure you're a hockey player? You'd make a great writer."

He leans down, his pale pink lips a breath away from my own. "I'm a man of many talents, Shortcake. You want to find out more of them?"

"Yes," I hum, "I'd like that very much."
"Then strip. I want to shave your legs for you."

CHAPTER SIX

Leo

HER EYES BUG OUT of her head in disbelief. "You want to shave my legs?" she asks.

I place my hands on her ample hips, pulling her pelvis up into me. "Let's get slippery, Shortcake."

She thinks for a second before saying, "Nobody has ever shaved my legs before."

"Wow! They must be hairy then. Good thing I have more than one razor."

She scoffs and smacks my chest. "You know what I mean."

I kiss her nose. "Then I'm happy to be your first. Now strip. Or I'll haul you over my shoulder and show you how much I don't care about your hairy legs."

"So bossy."

"You have no idea, baby." *Just wait till I put her over my knee.*

She presses her lips together, body going taunt. I have no idea where her sexual experience or preferences lie, which we'll have to talk about while we eat dinner. But I figure shaving her legs is a great introduction to a little bit of kink and an orgasm appetizer or two. No need for safe words...yet.

"You just want me to take my clothes off?" she asks.

I run a finger along her waistband slowly. "Unless you need help."

She pauses a moment, then says, "I think I might."

With a sly smile, I waste no time and move to unbutton her jeans before she has a chance to change her mind. The sound of her zipper fills the bathroom. Between that and our heavy breathing, it's an erotic soundtrack.

"Have I mentioned that granny panties turn me on?" I ask her.

"You haven't," she breathes out, the warm air tickling my lips.

I press my hard cock into her lower belly.

"I want to know what color they are." I kiss her jawline, slipping my tongue along the salty skin there. "And you know what else I want to know?"

"What?" she replies breathlessly.

"If they're soaked for me."

Before she can respond, I move one of my hands to her neck and pull her lips to mine roughly. We collide, her grip finding my hips so she can flatten us together. I'm not slow like I wanted myself to be at first; instead, I devour her, her air becoming mine as she opens her mouth to me. The way she kisses, any thoughts of propriety fly out the window. This woman knows how to use her mouth, and together we're a fire on a cold winter's night, burning and snapping in a symphony of heat and flame.

Riley moans as I slide my tongue against hers, tangling them together. She tastes like the drink Jace made us: cranberry with the earthy aftertaste of rosemary. Sweet and perfect. I pull back slightly and nip at her bottom lip, then dive back in for another taste, and another. My hand slips inside the front of her pants, and I press my knuckle gently against the wet fabric of her panties.

"Oh, fuck!" she cries, her body jolting at my touch.

I swallow her sounds, hoping Jace can hear us all the way in the kitchen. If I were him, I'd be at the door watching, but he can be more of a gentleman than me. She grabs the front of my shirt with one hand and pulls me impossibly closer, her lips seeking more contact. I oblige her, moving my fingers from her neck to the tresses of her sunset hair as I gently tease the panty-clad seam of her sex.

We make out until my lips start to go numb, and I forget where Riley ends and I begin. Her form is now pliant against mine, and I know if I were to come in skin-to-skin contact with her clit, she'd combust. Reluctantly, I pull back, removing my hand from her pants and bringing my damp fingers to my lips.

She watches as my tongue darts out to lick the flavor there.

"I was right," I say.

"About what?" she asks, her voice heady with sex.

"You taste like strawberries." A breathy laugh leaves her, and I can't resist giving her another lingering kiss. When I'm done, I take a step back so I can undress her this time. I have a job to do, after all. I can't get distracted, even if that was one of the best kisses of my life. I can't wait for Jace to experience her touch and taste. He's going to want to hold her hostage until after the New Year. Which I would one hundred percent endorse.

"You're really going to shave my legs?" she asks, disbelief still in her question.

I hum, lowering to my knees so I can push her pants down. They're tight, and with her body now heated, they're hard to get off. She wiggles her hips to help me, amused sounds spilling from her lips as the pants get stuck.

"Put your hands on my shoulders," I tell her.

"Yes, Sir." Her tone is teasing, but my entire body thrums at her words.

"Call me that again, Riley, and I may have Jace tie you to my bed all night so I can hear you call me Sir while I make you come till Christmas morning."

Her hands go to my shoulders, pussy moving closer to my face. It gives me the greenlight that she'd be into that, too. Fuck only one night with this woman; I want to keep her.

When I peel her pants all the way down, revealing lush thighs I want to sink my teeth into, I come face-to-face with her weeping light pink fabric-covered pussy. Her hands squeeze my shoulders and my gaze flicks back to hers. She's a bit nervous, and I think it's only because she's embarrassed about her damn underwear and the slight amount of hair I can see on her legs. It's ludicrous. I fuck all sorts of people with varying degrees of body hair. And it's not like Jace and I shave all the hair on our bodies. But I understand it's different for a lot of the population. I wish I could tell her society's ideal body standards aren't my game, but I know that wouldn't help her discomfort.

I lean forward and kiss her clit through the fabric, loving the way her breath hitches and her nails dig into my muscles. I do it again before moving my hands up the swell of her hips. When I reach the band that's digging into the skin of her mid-waist, I have the desire to kill whoever created these for women. I'm not even wearing them, but they can't be comfortable with how fucking tight they are. I'm going to make it my personal mission to kiss away any red marks that reside on her body. The only marks I want on her skin going forward are ones that Jace and I put on her.

Her voice is tense as she asks, "They're bad, aren't they?"

I push my hands under the elastic, her body shuddering at the contact of my fingers on the sensitive skin there. "They're way too tight, but I kind of like them."

She exhales a breathy laugh. "You're lying."

I pull them down inch by inch, my nails teasing her skin as I do. "If you're wearing them, I like them."

Riley looks down, a soft expression on her face along with a hint of sadness. A woman like her shouldn't have that look. And I bet it's all Chad-hole's fault.

I make sure to keep eye contact with her as I pull them all the way down, having her step out of them like she did her pants. The scent of her arousal hits me and I salivate. It's been a hot-minute since I ate a woman out, and while I love the salty taste of Jace on my tongue, this is what I crave right now. But I'm going to be a good boy and wait, because I have a job to do first.

I stand, loving the way I still tower over her despite her height. When she goes to say something, probably about the granny panties or her stubbly legs—or the way I noticed her pussy hair glistening with need for me, I put a finger to her lips. "Let me take care of you, Shortcake. Now arms up."

Those pine eyes stay on me as she does what she's told without hesitation. Good, she's relaxing a bit. I pull the sweater off, tossing it to the floor before making quick work of her simple beige underwire bra. I stand back to get a look at the lovely creature before me. She's plush everywhere, and her tits are large and heavy with nipples pert and wholly ready for my lips. I love the way her snowflake necklace still shines between her cleavage, so I decide to leave it on for decoration.

"How would you like to do this, shower or bath?" I ask.

She bites her lower lip, eyeing her options. When she catches sight of the bench in the rainforest shower, I know her answer. "Shower. It would be nice to wash up, too. I hate feeling like an airport. Also, I ran my ass through that terminal." Her nose scrunches a little at that.

Fuck, she's cute. "One shave and shower coming up."

I make quick work of turning the shower on and adjusting the temp so it's not too hot. "There's shampoo and whatever else you'd like inside. I promise that none of it smells like Old Spice." I grin at her. "Why don't you hop in and I'll gather some shaving supplies?"

Riley nods shyly, covering herself a bit as she moves into the shower. It's sweet that she's so shy after I just undressed her. But by the end of tonight, I'll have her walking around like a nudist. While she sighs at the warm water pounding on her skin, I get to work finding everything I need, including a fun surprise.

CHAPTER SEVEN

Riley

LUCAS MCKNIGHT WAS ON his knees in front of me. Undressing me, touching me. And that kiss!

Maybe I got on the plane and it crashed. Could this be my heaven? Or maybe I'm in a coma? Regardless, this is the sexiest night of my life, and no orgasms or dicks have been had yet. I smile to myself and glance at Lucas's figure rustling around in some cabinets through the frosted glass. When he steps out of the bathroom for "more supplies," I make quick work of scrubbing certain parts of me.

His soap smells herbal, and it helps relax my nerves a bit. Not to mention this shower. It's one of those fancy ones you only get to experience if you're rich as hell. It's practically massaging away all the tension in my body.

Just as I'm rinsing the conditioner from my hair, the glass door opens and Lucas steps in carrying a few things, one of them purple and oddly shaped. I don't keep my eyes on whatever it is, because he's buck-ass naked. I mean, I guess we're in a shower, so what would I expect him to do, wear a Speedo?

He stops when our eyes connect, his lips curving slowly into a sexy smile. "Ready for me?"

I can't help it. My eyes drop down his body, and I'm mesmerized by the water splashing onto his fair skin and dripping down his muscular form. When I reach his cock, I swear I stop breathing. It's not fully hard, but it's huge. Jesus, how does this man walk?

Lucas swaggers toward me and I can't take my eyes off It—I mean, him. That's going to be inside me at some point tonight. Will it even fit?

"It'll fit," he says, echoing my thoughts.

I wipe water from my eyes, and if my skin wasn't already red from the shower, it is now. "How did you know that's what I was thinking?" I huff.

He backs me up toward the bench that's just outside of the direct spray, looking down at me with amusement and a sexy cockiness only a man like him can have. "I've seen that look before. And trust me when I say you'll be fine. More than fine."

When he leans forward to lick some of the water from my cheek, it stuns me. This man really is something else. I've never met anyone like him, and I don't think I ever will again.

"Now let's not waste any more time, Shortcake."

He sets his supplies down on the bench, and when I get a closer look at the purple item, I know what it is. Never in my life have I had one inside me, despite my impressive sex toy collection. I may not own a butt plug, but I've seen plenty of them. Images of Jace and Lucas taking me at the same time fill my mind. Jace isn't small either, at least from the outline I could see through his sweats, which means I'm going to be stuffed full. My inner walls clench around nothing, and a jolt of pleasure shoots through me.

As if he just read my mind again, Lucas picks up the plug. "I take it you know what this is?"

"I do."

"Have you ever done anal before?

I shake my head. "It never happened during past relationships. And Chad wanted to, but I couldn't with him. It didn't feel right, considering he'd never try things I wanted."

"But you feel comfortable doing it with a man you just met?" There's absolutely no judgement in his tone, just curiosity.

Feeling brave, which I'll blame the alcohol and hormones for, I say, "Men. With men I just met."

That beautiful one-dimpled smile practically fills the room. "I think we were meant to meet each other tonight, Riley." He kisses my cheek, then sucks on my neck. "Now be a good girl and turn around. I need that pretty hole of yours nice and stretched for us."

My pussy floods, a strangled noise leaving my lips. Lucas only smiles wider as he makes a little twirling motion with his finger, and I do as he says.

"Place your hands on the wall, then just relax. It will feel strange at first, but you'll adjust."

I turn my head so I can look at him over my shoulder. "I trust you."

His icy gaze doesn't leave mine. For a second I think he's about to say something, but then he kisses my shoulder so tenderly it has my insides melting. He glides his hands down my back and to my ass. When his fingers start to probe the tight ring between my cheeks, a sharp gasp leaves my open mouth at the same time one of his hands comes down on my bottom. The sound of his slap on my wet skin echoes through the stall.

"Oh, fuck!" I cry out, my ass arching closer to him when logically I should want to draw it back.

"Oh," he observes, rubbing the skin he just punished. "Somebody likes that."

I try to answer, but he brings his hand down on the other cheek. I release another cry right as he slaps me twice more on each side. I swear my clit pulses from the act alone.

"You're so beautiful, Riley." My name on his lips has me cursing quietly. "Especially with my handprints on your ass. I can't wait to make you our little cock slut tonight."

"Oh god, yes," I whine, my voice not sounding like mine. "I want that."

He bites my earlobe. "Good. Because I think I'd die if you walked away right now. My cock is so hard from you."

I reach back and brush my fingertips against his steel length. In a second flat, his hand is around mine, keeping me away from my prize, while he pulls my wet hair back hard in his other fist. I gasp at the new sensations running though me. I don't know who this adventurous Riley is, but I should have let her come out to play sooner. I'm so turned on I can't think straight.

He tuts. "No touching. You won't deter me from my task. Got it?"

I remember his words earlier, so I answer with a breathy, "Yes, Sir."

He purrs. "Are you sure you haven't done this before?"

I shake my head.

"Just a good little slut then. Now I know why Santa sent you to me. Or was it Krampus?" He winks. "Now put your forehead on the wall and keep that sweet ass out."

With no reservations, I do as he asks, enjoying how he hums his approval. The faint sound of a cap opening hits my ears before the wet tip of the plug is at my entrance.

"It may burn a bit at first," he explains, his voice soothing, "but don't fight the feeling. Just relax and let me ease it in."

Lucas open-mouth kisses my neck and places one hand on my low hip so he can press the object inward. Immediately my body does what he told me not to do, but he's right there, his breath hot against my ear as he coaches me through the new sensation.

"Good fucking girl." He strokes the skin of my hip. "You take my plug so well. It's almost all in."

I let out a keening sound as the rest of it breaches my ass. It's an odd feeling. I don't feel super full, but it feels heavy. Like a small stretching weight that's not wholly unpleasant.

With a final kiss on my shoulder, Lucas spins me around so his hard cock is on my stomach. His wet body slides against mine, and I swear he looks like a God with the way the steam from the shower frames his muscular form.

"Now sit on the bench, Shortcake," he commands. "I don't know how much longer I can keep from tasting your sweet pussy."

My body tingles. Why did I care if my legs were hairy again? I want to go back on my request. But he's on a mission now. One I don't think I'll be able to keep him from. When I sit on the bench, my eyes widen at the feeling of the plug inside me.

He snickers. "Standing up is much easier. But I want you to feel the plug stretching you while I shave your legs. I want you to imagine what it will feel like to have Jace and me taking turns inside this amazing ass." He taps my clit. "And this greedy pussy."

"You have such a dirty mouth."

His eyes darken. "The better to eat you with, my dear."

With another brush of his fingers along my sex, he grabs a can of shaving cream, then kneels down on the tiled shower floor. It can't be comfortable, but he doesn't seem to care. He takes one of my legs and props it on his shoulder, my pussy once again level with his face. Even though my body is wet, it's very clear how turned on I am. He only smiles to himself as he gets to work, putting a generous amount of shaving cream in his hand before lathering it across my skin.

I'm fascinated by the concentration settling on his face. He brings a razor to the top of my knee and swipes away the white clouds in perfect lines. It's super cute, and emotion constricts my chest at how much care he's putting into this. The moment almost makes me forget about the intrusion in my ass. *Almost*.

A small groan escapes my lips as the plug hits a spot inside me that sends a jolt down my spine.

Lucas puts those ice blue eyes on me. "Feeling it, Shortcake?"

"It feels...interesting."

He releases a sound of satisfaction as he swipes more of the shaving cream away until my lower leg is done, and he moves to my upper thigh. As his masculine hands work, I fall into a sort of trance. His long fingers gripping my leg in support, the veins in his arm bulging slightly, and the water droplets clinging to his skin all have me stunned. I can't help the image that follows of those digits inside me. One time, I watched a porn video where the guy made the girl squirt just from his fingers. It was filthy and hot. I asked Chad if he would try it, but he said he wasn't into that. He always was a neat freak.

My mind is jolted from its shitty memory as a soft, unexpected kiss graces my thigh. Lucas's smile reassures me as his hands glide down my now smooth leg, effortlessly moving to the next.

Each soothing touch of his hands transports me to a different plane. When he runs the razor gracefully along my leg, the tingle of the shaving cream and the stainless-steel edge of the blades leave a lingering buzz of sensation that zings all the way to my core.

Lucas locks eyes with me once more, his pupils now a shade darker. The flush of heat on his skin mirrors the way my insides feel. My gaze drifts down, and I see his cock standing at attention, the skin dark red with arousal. It only intensifies my desire for him. In a deliberate motion, he leans forward to place gentle kisses along the freshly shaved skin, igniting a trail of electricity wherever his lips touch. He smooths more cream onto my thigh, his eyes fixed on me. The hunger and adoration in them has that unfamiliar emotion clenching in my chest again.

As his fingers glide closer and closer to my damp center, I let myself settle into all the feelings he's invoking in me, which only makes me more aware of the plug seated in my ass. In a way, I'm starting to enjoy it. Lucas squeezes my knee, then runs his strong hands over my now hairless legs.

"All done, Shortcake. Let's rinse you off."

Aware that I'm in some kind of blissful trance, he pulls me off the bench until our bodies are melded together and his cock rests against my belly. The skin is hot and silken, sending a tremor through my body. Wanting to feel more of him, I move a bit so there's a few seconds of delicious friction. Lucas groans, then grabs my jaw roughly, kissing me with an open mouth.

The kiss is chaotic, as if he's on the brink of losing control. His mouth is hot and stokes the needy fire that he's lit inside me. My hands wrap around his back and I score my nails against the muscular grooves of his shoulders. He hisses into my mouth and kisses me even deeper, my hips thrusting against his slick body as he digs his fingers into the skin of my ass. Just when I think we may end up fucking on the shower floor, he stops the kiss and taps the plug in my ass.

"Oh, Lucas!" I cry out. He does it again, and my head falls forward on his chest.

"That's what happens when you play with fire, Riley."

I whimper, a sound I didn't even know I could make. He only chuckles at my half-assed complaint, then pulls us under the lukewarm spray to hopefully finish what he's started.

CHAPTER EIGHT

Leo

RILEY'S GREEN EYES STARE up at me from beneath the spray of the shower. Her blown-out pupils and the shortness of her breath tell me all I need to know—that she's hanging on by a thread. The feeling is mutual. I never thought the act of shaving a woman's legs could bring me closer to God, or in this case the goddess known as Riley's pussy, but I'm ready to worship the fuck out of it.

I span my palms on the globes of her ass, spreading her cheeks wide to stimulate the plug inside her. The sexy noise that leaves her mouth has me doing it again before I pull away and spank each cheek in tandem. Her head falls into me as she cries out. I almost abandon my plans to eat her out in favor of fucking her, but I need to taste her before I starve.

I lift Riley's chin and brush away some of the hair from her face. When I brought her under the shower spray, I intended to wash away the residue of the shaving cream and clean myself up quickly. But fuck that. I cup her round face in my hands and bring my mouth to hers again. She opens for me immediately, letting me tongue-fuck her mouth until she's practically vibrating in my arms. I'm so caught up in the way she tastes that I don't notice her hand near my cock until it's wrapping around my shaft.

"Oh fuck, yes," I grunt, dropping my gaze to watch her fist my length.

"You're so big I can't even fit my whole hand around you," she says in wonder.

I curse again as she demonstrates her findings by trying to squeeze the life out of me. I manage to keep it together as she grips me in varying degrees of pressure, almost as if she's taking mental notes of what I respond to best. I usually like it hard and rough, but her delicate touch is doing something to me. Maybe I've gotten so used to Jace's hands that I've forgotten how gentle can be just as arousing. When her fingers brush over the delicate head, I almost lose it. I shoot a hand out to stop her movements.

"Did you not like that?" Her voice sounds hurt.

"The opposite."

"Then why did you make me stop?"

"Because," I move us so she's now pushed up against the shower wall, "I want to taste that pretty pussy." I lower myself to the ground, my eyes now level with my appetizer. "And I always get what I want."

Her chuckle dies on her lips as my mouth descends, a curse leaving her as I use my fingers to spread her wide and suck on her straining clit.

I vibrate in delight when her arousal fills my mouth. She's tangy and sweet, only enforcing that Shortcake is the perfect nickname for her. I lap at her folds and gently bite the skin there. I hear her head thump back against the wall, her hips pressing forward so I'm buried between her thighs.

"Hold on to me, baby," I murmur. "I don't want you to slip."

She does as she's told, but instead of placing her hands on my shoulders, she secures them to the back of my head to hold me in place while I eat her out and suck her clit between my lips. When the blunt edges of her white painted nails dig into my scalp, my dick throbs painfully and I almost come.

"Oh my god, Lucas!" she screams.

My cock deflates a bit at the sound of my brother's name on her lips. I'm a fucking idiot, but there's nothing I can do about it now. I'm too far down that rabbit hole. Trying to put it out of my mind, I focus on the task at hand. I swirl my tongue around her swollen nub before making little flicking motions over it. She makes sweet noises as I continue my assault, slowly dragging one of my hands from her hip to join in on the fun.

"Do you want my fingers, Shortcake?" I ask between licks and sucks.

She gazes down at me through hooded eyes and nods.

"Use your words." I slap her clit lightly for punctuation.

"Fuck, yes! Please, Sir. Fuck me with your fingers."

Okay, that brings my dick back to life.

I give her a playful glare. "I love it when you say *please.*"

My lips seal back over her as I seek out her warm opening. She's so incredibly wet and slippery, I want to spend hours down here exploring and seeing how many times I can make her orgasm.

When I swipe my fingers around her sensitive entrance, she makes a pleading noise that has me plunging one long finger in, and then another. When I feel how snug she is, I let out my own noise of pleasure around her clit. Her pussy is going to squeeze my cock so hard. I can't fucking wait.

"Your pussy is perfect, Riley. So fucking hot and tight. Especially with this." I push my fingers against the plug from inside her and stroke downwards. Riley cries out, her hands gripping me so fucking tight that if my lips were still attached to her clit, I'd probably be suffocating. Not that I'd mind. Ask any person who loves pussy, and I'm sure they'd say it's a good way to die.

"Do you want me to stop?" I tease.

She pins me with a darkened stare. "Don't stop, don't ever stop."

My ego inflates as I plunge my fingers in and out of her wetness, lapping at her sex with renewed vigor. I love her like this, totally at my mercy, skin wet and flushed. The steam from the shower makes me feel like we're inside our own bubble, and all that matters to me right now is making her come so hard that she almost passes out.

To get more leverage, I take one of her legs and drape it over my shoulder, having her hold on to me for dear life as I move my fingers faster and quicker inside her. At the new position, the plug in her ass shifts a bit and she turns into a garbled mess of gibberish. Her mouth opens and her head falls back. I wish I could capture her expression as I eat and finger-fuck the life out of her. Maybe I'll get some art commissioned so I can remember what it's like to worship her pussy forever.

"Come for me, Shortcake. Come all over my hand like the good little slut you are."

At my vulgar words, her body tenses. For a second I think I've gone too far, but then she shatters. Her inner walls clench around my fingers, squeezing them as she rides out her orgasm. To prolong her pleasure, I wrap my lips around the sensitive bud and suck.

"Oh shit, oh God!" she screams, her voice echoing through the shower. Her fingers dig further into my scalp as the aftershocks of her release wrack through her body. She looks beautiful in the throes of her pleasure. I can't wait to watch her come again with Jace while I witness every single moment.

After I'm sure she won't fall over, I give her clit a delicate kiss before standing. It takes only a split second for her to launch herself at me. Her lips attack mine with vigor, not caring that I'm covered in her arousal. I can feel my cock begging for attention at the dirty action, but it will have to calm the fuck down because I'm enjoying the way Riley's pliant body feels against mine. Her kisses are hurried, but focused. In a way, it's like we've been doing this for years.

When her pruned fingertips brush against the muscles of my back, I force myself to pull away. Her lips are puffy and her cheeks are red with heat. While I could keep kissing her all night, Jace is waiting for us. I'm impressed he hasn't come to make sure we're still alive—though I'm sure he heard Riley's screams and is probably rock hard from it.

"That was," she exhales an astonished breath, "that was…I don't even know what that was."

"You came hard. It was fucking hot."

She laughs shyly, then trails her hand toward my cock. I let out a little tsk. "Not so fast." I take her wrist and kiss the inside of it. "You'll take care of me later, but right now we need to get out of this shower and eat dinner. Jace is getting jealous."

She bites her lower lip, eyes glancing back. "What about the plug?"

I reach behind her and tap it. "That stays in, baby."

Chapter Nine

Jace

They've been in that shower for an hour, and my cock is jealous. Okay, not just my cock.

I almost joined them, but I want Riley to feel comfortable with us. If you've never been with two people at once, it can be a lot. She also came home with Leo and didn't really grasp that she could have the two for one option. I think it was a good idea for him to warm her up, make sure she feels safe before we introduce more.

There's also the reality that Leo and I are *a lot* to handle, especially together. We like it rough and wild more than slow and languid. My thoughts drift to a night earlier this year when he brought home a spreader bar from some new sex shop he'd visited downtown. I'd spent the night in a bind, letting him do whatever the hell he wanted to me. I think I came so many times my come literally dried out. I was exhausted for days after.

It was worth it though. With my eyes closed, I can feel the phantom touch of his strong hands massaging my sore muscles afterward. Leo may be rough, but he also likes to kiss things better. A slow smile touches my lips, and my cock jumps to life. It was such a hot night that now I want to do it again. Maybe with a certain curvy woman there to watch.

The oven timer pings, jolting me back to present time. I push away the image and whatever the hell it means that I'm thinking of Riley with us before we've done anything by taking a few calming breaths. I've managed to scrounge up a meal for the three of us. It was just by luck that I'd planned to cook a nice steak dinner and had bought a pack of two large bone-in ribeyes. I hope Riley likes red meat.

I pull out potatoes and asparagus from the oven, enjoying the smell of garlic and spices as it hits my nose. My stomach growls. I hope they hurry up so we can eat while it's hot. I was about to cook at six o'clock when I found out Leo would need a ride home, and now it's just after nine, so, I'm starved.

"Smells delicious."

My head whips around at Riley's voice. Her hair is wet, her skin a lovely shade of pink from the shower. She looks sexy in a simple pair of black leggings and a green V-neck sweater that hugs every dip and valley of her body. Though I miss the Christmas getup from before, this one gives me a better idea of what she has under her clothes.

"Thanks. I hope you like steak and potatoes." I smile, setting the tray of hot food on the island.

"I'm a vegetarian, actually."

I swear my heart stops until I see a crack of a smile appear. She giggles. "I'm kidding."

"Good one, Riley. You had me going for a split second."

"I can be funny sometimes."

My gut tells me that's a lie. I bet this girl's got jokes for days. "Would you like a drink? I have a nice red wine that will go well with dinner."

"That sounds perfect. Thanks, Jace."

I grab the bottle and pour a glass for her, doing the same for Leo since I know he'll want one when he's done making himself pretty for Riley. He's probably putting on some expensive moisturizer as we speak. That man loves to look put together, even in the comfort of his own home.

"Here you go." I hand her the generous pour, enjoying the way her eyes glitter as she smiles.

She holds up her glass, so I grab mine off the counter. "Cheers to new friends," she says.

I give her a cool smile. "To new friends. And to new adventures."

She holds my stare, the nervous woman from earlier gone from view. "And to new adventures," she echoes.

We both take a sip of the dry liquid just as I hear Leo, or should I say Lucas, approach. His feet pad softly against the hardwood floors as his sexy body comes into view. He's wearing the same outfit he changed into before he 'helped' Riley in the shower, except I can one-hundred percent tell he's gone commando under his gray sweats. More blood rushes to my lower half when I see the hefty outline of my favorite toy. I remind myself we have dinner to eat before we get to the dessert, but it's fun to look and anticipate what will happen afterward.

"It smells fantastic in here, J." He kisses Riley on the forehead as he reaches for the unclaimed glass of wine on the counter. At his affection, she shifts in her chair, eyes glossing over like she's recalling everything that happened in the bathroom.

"Thanks..." I let my eyes wander Leo's form again, then linger on Riley's perfect chest. "Dinner is ready if you both want to sit down. I set up the dining room."

Leo licks his lips at my attention before he raises a questioning eyebrow at me. "Wow. Maybe I should stay home for Christmas more often. We never use the dining room for meals."

I shrug. "Seems like the perfect occasion to use it for something other than work or lewd acts."

He gives me a lazy grin and I shoot him one back. I know I've got him thinking about the other night when I fucked him on the fancy glass table to stop him from working late. I went so hard I thought the table would shatter. Turns out, that thing is worth its weight in gold. Maybe we'll spread Riley on top of it after we eat. Leo probably wouldn't be opposed to adding another lewd act to the bank.

"You're a deviant." He chuckles, throwing a wink to Riley as she watches us with curiosity. I'm sure she's wondering what we did in the dining room exactly, but that's a story for another time.

"You wouldn't have me any other way," I say to Leo. "Now you two go. I'll be right behind you."

As Leo walks away with Riley on his arm, I think he says "all night" under his breath in what I know is a reference to me being behind him. The promise of it doesn't help my hard dick situation, but I try to ignore it. I worked too hard on this food, and we do need sustenance for the activities to come.

Laughter flitters from the dining room into the kitchen as I make our plates. With the snow falling outside, the Christmas lights illuminating the room, and the two of them waiting for me, a contented warmth settles in my stomach. I may have just met Riley, but she's already fitting in with us. For the last couple of years, Leo and I have become more exclusive than he realizes. We work together, sleep together, and often even travel together. Sure, we have sexual partners coming in and out, but nothing serious. And it's been fewer and fewer partners in the last year.

I stay at his place a lot too, so much in fact I've come to wonder why I even have my own place. Maybe things haven't changed because it's gotten to the point of "if it's not broke, don't fix it," which is usually fine. I hadn't really thought much about this subject in a while since we've been so busy, but Riley's question about us being together has my brain turning back to the thoughts I've buried over the years.

I take a sip of wine and clear my mind. Tonight is not the night to dredge up complicated shit. It's a night to celebrate good 'ole St. Nick and cozy up with two beautiful people. So I grab our plates, using my ex-server skills to balance the three meals. When I turn into the large formal dining room, I expect to find them still smiling and laughing at each other. Instead, I discover Leo kissing the life out of Riley. Neither of them notices me at first, but I don't mind. I stand still and enjoy the show for a few seconds.

Leo has always been an amazing kisser. The first time we crossed the line from friends and coworkers to friends and coworkers with benefits, he was the one to make the move. I'd known since college that Leo is pansexual, but I didn't tell him I'm bisexual until graduation. My mom is Native Hawaiian and my dad is Native Hawaiian and Samoan. Both were raised Mormon in the LDS Church, which means I was too. It's hard for people to believe that when I tell them, but Mormonism is more common in Polynesian culture than they realize. When you tell people Hawaii has the highest concentration of Latter-day Saints of U.S. states that do not border Utah, they tend to gape in surprise. That's why it took me leaving my home and taking time to figure my shit out in college to be able to really express who I am.

When I came out to Leo, he was excited for me. I think he always knew, since I wasn't exactly trying to hide it per se, but I was glad he gave me the space to explore. It still took years for us to cross the line, not because there wasn't chemistry there, but we were both so busy trying to make a name for ourselves, and then he started handling his brother's career. I think there was also a part of us that was too scared to ruin the friendship we have. Especially since we spend so much time together.

But eventually, I started dropping hints that I was interested. I'd be lying if I said I wasn't *always* interested and too chicken to say anything. I had a silly crush on him even before we met. He was the most popular and best hockey player on campus. There was a reason I was able to recite his stats to him the night we met—and it wasn't only because I wanted to be a sports agent after college. So when one night, years and years later, we got buzzed while working late and he kissed me...let's just say I ended up on my knees more than once that night.

A sexy moan from Riley reminds me where I am and that I'm holding our dinner. I clear my throat, and she gasps, pulling back from Leo's lips. He's got a cocky ass grin on his face when he makes eye contact with me, whereas Riley looks like her nickname. Given I just heard her come through several walls, it's amusing she's embarrassed I found her simply kissing. Hopefully, we'll help her get over that embarrassment quickly, though I admit I like it when her skin starts turning to the color of her hair. It's cute.

"Starting with dessert?" I ask Leo.

He wiggles his eyebrows like the horndog he is while Riley takes a large gulp of her wine. To change the subject from sexual innuendos, I place their plates of food down in front of them, then quickly grab my wine from the kitchen. I then take a seat at the head of the table so we form a L-shape. It also gives me direct access to Riley.

"Wow, Jace," she says in wonder. "I can't believe you did all this."

I wave away her praise. "I was planning to cook this meal for myself anyway. I just multiplied it."

She reaches over to squeeze my hand. "Don't minimize it. This is incredible. I can't remember the last time anyone cooked for me."

Now I'm blushing. "Thanks, Riley."

She pulls her hand away and beams at Leo, who's ignoring his plate to moon at her. My friend is smitten. I'm trying to remember if I've ever seen him like this before, but I don't think I have. For as long as I've known him, I've seen him lust after people, but this? It's different. Most people would think that would make me jealous, but I've never been like that. I've always felt that you could love more than one person at once.

When Riley lifts her fork, Leo unglues his eyes from her to meet my stare. My heart flutters when the corners of his mouth curve into a small smile: one I only see when we're alone. It's also another reason I don't get jealous. What I have with him is unique and special to us. I give him my own "us only" smile back as he picks up his fork to take his first bite of steak. His eyes close and pure bliss erupts on his face.

"Goddamn, J," he says with a groan. "You know I love your meat, but this is A++."

Riley laughs, the sound a delight. I guess he couldn't stay away from the sexual innuendos for more than a few minutes.

"Thanks, I tried a new reverse sear method," I say.

"Sounds kinky," he teases.

"You're incorrigible."

His icy eyes sparkle mischievously as he closes his lips around another bite. I shift in my chair, still semi-hard from hearing and thinking about their shower activities for the last hour. He knows it too; that's why he's looking at me like he can't wait to eat me instead of dinner.

"So, Riley," I say, "tell us more about yourself."

She swallows and sips her wine. "What do you want to know?"

"The usual. How old are you, where did you grow up, have you ever been fucked by two men at the same time before?"

Riley almost spits out her wine, and for a second I feel bad for being so blunt. But between Leo's innuendos, sexy stares, and watching them kiss, I'm ready to get to the heart of why we're all here.

"Jesus, Jace," Leo scolds, rubbing Riley's back as she coughs, although the twinkle in his eye tells me he's not mad about my question. Two can play at this game.

Riley wipes her mouth with a napkin. "I have to say I've never been asked that question, let alone at a dinner table, but I've also never been in this situation, either."

My gaze intensifies as I make eye contact with her. "So? Will you answer."

"I just turned thirty last month, I grew up in Seattle, and no, I've never had sex with two men at the same time before. I've also never had a threesome of any variety." Her eyes turn hazy for a moment, like she's thinking about something.

"But you've thought about it?" I ask, and she blushes. I continue, "If this is making you uncomfortable, I can stop."

She shakes her head. "I mean, if I can't talk about sex, I probably shouldn't be having it. Let alone with two sexy men."

Leo and I both let out a breathy laugh.

"Isn't that what they used to say to us in school?" I ask.

"I think so." She bites into a potato. Once she finishes, she says, "But to answer your question—yes, I've imagined it before. I don't know many women who haven't. But I can't say it's something I think about often, until tonight, that is."

I peer at her over the brim of my wine glass. "Does it make you nervous?

Riley shifts in her chair, wincing a little as she does. Leo pays close attention to the movement, biting his lip as if he's trying to stop a smile from forming. That's when I remember the controller I have in my pocket. Leo handed it to me with a wink before he returned to Riley in the shower. He didn't inform me of what he planned to do to her in there, but when he gave me the little black object, it didn't take me long to figure out who would be wearing the plug that it controls.

Riley clears her throat delicately. "A little nervous. But after my shower, I'm feeling more relaxed."

"Good, because I have another question for you." I hum as my finger hovers over the power button of the controller. "Can I play with you a bit?"

Her eyes widen. She's unsure of what I mean. Leo watches us in silence.

"You'll be safe," I say. "And I promise, it will feel good. If it doesn't, you can tell me to stop." I give her a warm smile and enjoy the way her breath hitches and her hand clenches around her fork.

"Okay."

"I need a yes, Riley," I say. My words are heavy and demanding in a way that has her squirming a bit.

After a moment, she dips her head. "Yes. You can play."

Leo releases a small groan at her response, and Riley's eyes dart to meet his. I use the opportunity of her distraction to have my fun. As soon as my hand hits what I know is the little plus button, Riley cries out. Leo's face turns lustful as he watches Riley writhe, her hands reaching out to grip the edge of the table. I press the button again, increasing the vibrations just a bit.

"Oh my god," she pants. "It's vibrating."

Leo strokes his hand down Riley's back. "Sorry, Shortcake. I left that little part out."

I lean back in my chair, pressing the button one more time just to see what she does.

"Oh fuck!" Her voice is a whine, one that says she likes it, and her protests are just a knee jerk reaction. Her hands continue to grip the table as her darkened eyes lock on mine.

"Jace—" She pauses to take a breath, and I hit the plus button to add little pulses. Another cry escapes her lips, but she doesn't tell me to stop, which I take as a good sign. I decide to go a little further with it and hit the setting that makes it move in an edging pattern while I take another bite of steak. I want her to get lost in the sensations, to feel helpless and out of control. My nonchalant behavior is part of letting her know that I have her in the palm of my hand.

As I chew slowly, I can feel her eyes on me. If I looked into them right now I'm sure I'd see a half-assed plea for me to stop. But at the same time, she wants this. Wants to feel out of control. And I want to draw her pleasure out. As Leo knows, instant gratification isn't really my thing. I could wait to orgasm for hours, which is super helpful when you're playing with partners in scenes or in groups.

"Jace," she says. "It feels..." Her voice fades, and when I look up, her eyes are squeezed shut.

"What does it feel like?" Leo asks. "Use your words, Shortcake." At Leo's Dom voice, my cock throbs. *Fuck*. He's so sexy when he gets all demanding.

"It feels," Riley moans, "intense."

Leo brushes a lock of drying hair from her neck and kisses the skin he finds there. "Intense good or bad?"

She huffs a strangled laugh. "G-good, but it's—" I turn it up again. Riley's head falls back and she curses. "Jace, please."

I put my fork down. "Please what, Riley baby?"

"Please, turn it off or—" She moans again. "Or I might explode."

I have to bite the inside of my cheek to keep myself from chuckling. Leo holds up a hand, his less than subtle way of telling me to turn it off. When I do, Riley slumps forward, taking several deep breaths.

"What do you say to Jace, Shortcake?" Leo asks, running his fingers through her hair until he's gently pulling it.

Riley moans. "Thank you, Sir."

Oh Jesus, she called me Sir. My eyes shoot to Leo, the shock obvious on my face. He's grinning like a cat who caught the canary. Now I want to know exactly what happened in that bathroom. My anticipation for tonight only grows at the knowledge that Riley is into what Leo and I like. They make me want to abandon the meal I worked so hard on and fuck them both until they don't remember their names.

I scoot forward and place my hand over the one Leo still has in Riley's hair near the base of her skull. Leo practically purrs as I dig my short nails into the back of his hand and turn Riley's face toward mine. I use my free hand to grasp her jaw.

"Good girl," I praise. Riley's sharp intake of breath only arouses me further. Her words have ignited the dominant beast inside me that's been dormant recently.

She stares at my mouth, then back up to my hazel eyes, licking her pretty lips. Fuck. It takes everything in me not to kiss her, but I want to tease her a bit longer.

"Now, let's finish our meal before it turns to ice," I say, releasing her jaw and Leo's hand before turning back to my plate as if nothing happened.

Leo exhales tensely, and I know his balls are drawn up tight. When we play together, we'll take turns topping each other. If we have multiple partners, sometimes we will top together. Though more often than not, he's the one that likes to dominate and I'm more than happy to oblige. I can't remember the last time I made him crawl to me; it's been at least a few months.

The base of my spine tingles at the prospect of owning him along with Riley—it sounds like the perfect Christmas gift. Of course, I'll let him top her too, but that doesn't mean I can't have my fun with them first. And judging by Leo's show just now, I think he wants me to take the lead. I know him better than I know myself, and vice versa. He's ready to let go for a bit. Thank fuck.

I put another piece of steak in my mouth and dare a glance at Riley. She's staring at her half-eaten plate, fingers still gripping the table. Leo's assessing her carefully, his hand now on her inner thigh. Eventually, her eyes blink and she shifts in her chair, no doubt trying to ease the fullness of the plug in her ass. I follow her movements as she picks up her fork and spears a piece of asparagus. She opens her mouth, her smiling eyes meeting mine. I watch with rapture as she slides the long green vegetable between her lips then playfully bites off the tip, making sure to show her straight white teeth as she does it.

The action has me laughing and shifting in my own chair.

This woman is trouble.

CHAPTER TEN

Leo

I CAN SEE SPARKS from the all the tension in the air. But it's not a bad kind of tension. It's the kind that has your toes curling and goosebumps breaking out across your skin. The kind that makes your cock hard or your pussy wet. The kind that makes you want to throw everything off the table and go at it for hours until one of you passes out.

Needless to say, it's my favorite kind of tension. However, it's making it incredibly hard (pun intended) to finish the beautiful meal Jace made. I'm so wound up after what just transpired between us that I don't even taste anything. But I'm going to finish the food regardless, because A) I need my strength for tonight, and B) Jace ordered it. Goddamn, that was hot. I love when Daddy Jace comes out to play, and it's been far too long since he has. Which I know is entirely my fault.

The memory of the night I discovered his Dom comes to mind. It was shortly after we started sleeping with each other. Since the day I met him, he knew I desired control in my life, and in the beginning, he always gave it to me. Then one night, I was in my head about something Lucas said to me about my injury and how amazing it would have been to be on the ice together in the NHL. Jace took matters into his own hands, tying me up for the first time that night, and before I knew it, he had me calling him Daddy as he fucked me raw. I never thought I had a Daddy kink, but Jace? It fits him.

With his thick 6'3" light brown form, nicely trimmed full beard, and his caring and protective demeanor, he makes the fantasy real. And as Riley will soon find out when he strips, he's covered in tattoos. It's sexy and downright sinful.

Let's just say that after that night, I did some serious self-exploration. Turns out, I'm more of a switch than I thought. And since then, I've done a lot of things that involve complete surrender. I enjoy it almost as much as I do ordering people around. Almost.

"More wine?" Jace asks, his deep voice making those goosebumps reappear on my arms.

I meet Jace's gaze and shake my head. "I'm good. Riley?"

She pushes her now empty plate away. "I think if I eat or drink anything else you'll have to roll me out of here. It was delicious, though." Her praise lights up Jace's angular face and it makes me happy.

"I'm glad you liked it." Jace wipes his mouth and facial hair, then addresses me. "Are you done, baby?"

My heart beats quicker at the pet name. He calls me that sometimes, but usually only during sex or when he's trying to get me to agree to something. He knows it's one of my weak spots.

"All done." My voice comes out breathy and laced with what I can only describe as anticipation.

Riley shifts in her chair and catches an eyeful of my straining cock. He's ready to come out to play, and she knows it. She moves her hand to my thigh, pulling her fingers along the fabric of my sweats until she delicately brushes them over my erection. My cock twitches beneath her touch.

I move her hand so it's fully over my hard length. "Are you ready for dessert, Riley?"

She bats her eyes demurely. "I've been ready since our shower."

I give her a cocky grin and turn to Jace. "Should we move this to the bedroom?"

Jace stands. "I have a better idea."

He uses his pointer and middle finger to beckon us to follow him. It's a bit comical how quickly Riley and I stand. I even stumble a bit in my haste.

We follow him through the dining room and back into the main living area until we reach my favorite room in the house, my "man cave." It's not really a man cave per se, but it's the space in my home I use the most when I need to relax. It's cozier than the living room with a large couch and attached chaise lounge. Even some fun bean bag chairs. There's a massive TV on the wall for watching sports and movies, including surround sound.

When Riley sees the large Fraser fir in the corner decorated to the nines, including a lit fireplace with stockings and holly, she gasps and claps her hands. "This room looks straight out of a Christmas movie!" she cheers.

She's not wrong. While normally this room is plain, Jace surprised me last month by having a professional decorator do the whole penthouse (though it was definitely for him more than me). And while every room in my place looks like what I would call "Christmas Classy," this room has lots of extra details and feels more like my parents' home in Seattle. The tree is covered in multi-colored lights instead of white, and different kinds of fun ornaments cover the branches while an oversized red and gold tree skirt sits around its base.

"I thought you'd like it." Jace smiles affectionately. He takes his place on the couch, stretching out on the attached oversized chaise lounge. He pats the cushion next to him and Riley doesn't hesitate to join him. Once she sits, he pulls her into his side until they're snuggling. It's sweet, there's an unknown emotion tugging inside me. I can't really say what it is, but it's nice. And fucking scary at the same time, especially considering Riley is only here for the night.

"Get over here," Jace's gravelly voice commands.

I startle a bit and realize I've been staring. "Sorry, you two are just so cute," I croon.

Jace huffs. "I'm not cute."

I try not to laugh as I settle myself on to the couch next to Riley, resting my hand on her thigh. I momentarily let the beauty of the room and the people in it fill me up and ground me. The lights are dimmed, and the air is warm and cozy. For a second, I wonder why I've been such a Scrooge about Christmas all these years. Because if this is what holidays are like, I could get behind celebrating more willingly.

Riley shifts, her actions revealing the same quiet contentment that I feel. Her sparkling gaze flashes to my lips, and I find myself unable to hold back any longer. I'm about to move my hand closer to her pussy to find out just how wet she is for us, but Jace's big hand stops me. "Did I say you could do that, *Lucas*?"

Riley doesn't notice the tone of dislike he has when he says my brother's name, because it sounds commanding. But I can hear the difference. When we make eye contact, his eyebrow is raised in question. He doesn't look angry, just ready to show me who's boss.

"You wanna play, Jace?" My voice holds a rawness, conveying the depth of my need for him.

He strokes the top of my hand with his thumb. "Do I have your permission?"

I let out a shaky breath. He's so hot when he gets like this. In the last few months we just grab each other and go at it, so this is a fun change. And it's all thanks to Riley's presence here. "You know you do," I tell him.

He nods, then turns his attention to Riley while keeping his hand over mine on her thigh. "What about you, Riley?" he asks. "Do we have your consent to do anything we want to you?"

She bites her lower lip. "Anything?"

He grins. "Within reason, of course."

She laughs nervously. "Yes, you have my consent. I trust you both. I was also tested recently, so I'm all good there."

Her words are a turn-on and I'm about ready to pounce. "We are, too."

Jace traces a finger down her arm sensually. "If anything makes you uncomfortable, or it's too much, say the word and everything stops. Understand?"

"I understand, Sir."

Jace places one of his thick fingers under her chin, giving her a sly grin that could drop panties within a mile radius. "You're already a natural, baby. But please, call me Daddy."

CHAPTER ELEVEN

Riley

I THINK MY LEGGINGS are soaked. No, not think. I *know* they are.

Out of all the requests to come out of Jace's mouth, asking me to call him Daddy wasn't anything I could have dreamed of. But the way he said it, and how he looks like he's ready to devour me—I'll call the man whatever he wants. I just need to feel him everywhere on and in my body.

Jace and Lucas are staring at me hungrily, waiting to see my reaction. They're both so aware of what they're asking of me, it's a huge turn-on. Chad and all my other exes always just took, I mean, they did have my consent but I always just gave in because I'm a people-pleaser. But I don't feel like that with these two. With them, I know they won't do anything I don't want, including if I asked Jace to let me call him by his name. The thought makes me happy.

I wet my lips, the men before me eyeing the movement of my tongue. "I understand...*Daddy.*"

Jace and Lucas let out a groan, but before I can do anything else, that buzzing in my ass starts again. It makes a pattern, moving at varying speeds, then pausing before starting again.

"Oh shit!" The sensation is intense, and my body is already on fire. I lean my head back against the couch as Lucas moves his hand toward my center. When I manage to look down, Jace still has his hand over Lucas's and is directing where it goes.

Observing the two manly hands one on top of the other, Jace's veins bulging as he grips Lucas, it's the stuff of dreams.

"Rub her clit," Jace commands Lucas, his voice gruff.

"Yes, Daddy," he answers, his tone completely serious.

I let out a whine at his words, my arousal increasing.

"You like when I call Jace 'Daddy?'" Lucas asks me.

I bite my lower lip and nod as his fingers rub me through the fabric of my leggings.

"What do you like about it?" Jace asks, tracing one of his thick fingers down my jaw.

I ping-pong my gaze between them, thinking of why it turns me on so much. In a way, the two of them are opposites, minus that they're both smoking hot. While Lucas has a pretty-boy charm, ice blue eyes, and a body that screams, "I eat protein shakes for lunch and work out seven days a week," Jace has a soft, round stomach, dark hazel eyes, and a beard that screams for you to sit on his face.

"Well?" Jace asks again, amusement in his tone.

"I like seeing someone like Lucas do what you say," I answer.

Jace presses Lucas's hand harder into my clit while at the same time upping the vibration in my ass. I try to stifle my cries as I squirm, but I'm held in place by Lucas's other hand.

Jace kisses my jaw. "What do you mean?"

I let out a shuddering breath. "Lucas was so dominant in the shower with me. I didn't expect this. It's...it's so hot."

"You like the idea of someone dominant being dominated, then?" Jace reflects, his breath tickling my ear.

"I guess?"

Jace lets out a soft chuckle. "Well, you're in luck, then. Because I'm the only one he calls Daddy."

My pussy pulses at his words, and I have the intrusive thought to yell, "flash flood warning!" but thankfully, I don't.

"What do you say we put on a show for our little slut, Daddy?" Lucas asks, his voice heady with sex and lust.

Jace stops the movements of Lucas's hand on my clit, and I make a desperate sound from the sudden loss. I don't miss the small smile he gets from hearing it, the torturous bastard.

"You trying to top me already, baby?" he asks Lucas.

Lucas shakes his head. "Just a little suggestion."

Jace releases a grunt that says he doesn't believe him, but when his gaze turns to me, I know his decision.

"You want to see me tell our pretty boy to suck my cock?"

"Fuck yes." The words are out of me before I can even think.

"You are a dirty slut, aren't you?" Jace affirms, his tone playful.

Oh boy. Forget the flash flood, it's a full on tidal wave down there now. I never thought being called a slut would turn me on, but they both say it as if it's a term of endearment instead of an insult.

Jace grips my jaw with a gentle force, his lips hovering over mine. *Fuck.* Who is this man? When I first met him, I thought he was just a sweet guy, like a puppy dog. But no, he's a wolf in sheep's clothing.

"Answer me, Riley, and I'll be nice and let you watch. If you don't, I'll blindfold you and make you listen while the plug in your ass eats you alive."

"Yes, Daddy. I'm a dirty little slut." The words come out so naturally I even surprise myself.

A growl of appreciation slips from his lips before he kisses me softly. "Good girl. Now watch closely."

He snaps his fingers and Lucas's warm body drops away from mine and onto the floor. I'm mesmerized as he expertly lands on his knees and looks at Jace with pure surrender and what I can only call love, though it seems deeper than that. I know these two say they're not "together, together," but as an outsider looking in, I'd call that horse shit.

"Now come up here and take my cock out," Jace commands him, his tone almost bored.

Lucas doesn't lose time. He joins Jace on the chaise lounge, kneeling between his now spread legs. He slides his palms up Jace's meaty thighs toward their destination. His movements are slow, agonizing, even. Jace grabs Lucas's chin and taps his cheek.

"No teasing, brat. Or I'll be forced to throat-fuck you with your hands tied behind your back."

My body grows heavy with arousal. Why did that image turn me on so much? Wow, I'm such a pervert and I had no idea. What are these men unleashing from inside me?

Lucas nods and Jace lets him get back to what he was doing. This time, his hands go to the band of Jace's sweatpants and he pulls them down inch by inch, revealing thighs decorated in traditional Polynesian tattoos, and what I can only call a monster cock. It's thick and long, the skin red and engorged with his arousal.

"Holy crap," I mutter, unable to form any other kind of words.

Lucas chuckles as Jace's bedroom eyes find mine. I try to imagine both men inside me and wonder if I might end up in the hospital by the end of the night. "*Serious internal injury from two large cocks*" is what my chart would say.

"Relax, beautiful," Jace says. The way he calls me beautiful has my body tingling. "What do you think that plug inside you is for?" With a sly grin, he leans back against the couch and turns his attention to Lucas. "Get to work, McKnight. I don't have all night."

Lucas jumps into action, using one of his hands to hold Jace's cock while his lips descend over the broad crown. Jace hisses and I watch as his length disappears past Lucas's lips.

"Fuck, baby. I love your mouth," Jace moans, moving one of his hands to brush a few strands of damp hair from Lucas's forehead. Then he strokes down his smooth square jaw. The action is sweet, yet so stunning I think I could come just from watching them. I mean, the vibrating plug helps, too, but these two are a sight to see. I've never watched men together before, but now I think I should've. It's beautiful. *They're beautiful.*

Lucas moves his hand up Jace's thick shaft, then twirls his tongue around the crown, his eyes staying on Jace's the whole time. Once he's developed a bit of a rhythm, Jace palms the back of Lucas's head and in one swift movement, pushes him down until over half of his cock is now in Lucas's mouth. Which I didn't even think was possible.

"That's it, baby," Jace goads. "Take Daddy's cock."

Lucas hums with pleasure and takes more of Jace down his throat. Lucas is really good, because he doesn't gag at all. I wonder how much of Jace's "monster" I could take in? Or how much of Lucas's. Maybe only half?

Jace's free hand lands on my thigh, pulling me from that interesting question.

"He's amazing, isn't he?" Jace asks.

"Yes, he is."

Lucas makes an approving noise, lapping up the praise. Then he cups Jace's balls and gives them a nice squeeze. I watch in rapture as the soft planes of Jace's face go taunt, his breath hitching as he moves Lucas's head down on his cock. The dirty sight has me shifting again, my body tingling and dying to be touched. I've gotten used to the buzzing in my ass, but I'm so wound up I could burst.

"Take off your clothes, Riley."

My head whips so I'm looking at Jace, his command zipping through me straight to my clit. He gives me a questioning look, as if he's wondering if I'm not going to do it. But after my experience with Lucas in the bathroom, and the show that's currently being put on for me, I don't feel so shy anymore. I get up, trying to ignore the plug in my ass and how wet my leggings are between my thighs.

With my eyes on Jace, I start to peel off my sweater. The moment is only made hotter by how he keeps moving Lucas's head up and down his cock like his own personal Fleshlight.

Once that's taken care of, I reach behind to unclasp my bra. When my breasts bounce free, Jace doesn't look down, but continues to hold eye contact with me. Though I see the way his body tenses, and how he moves Lucas's face harder down his cock.

The wet noises of spit and sucking spur me to finish my task. With quick movements, I remove my leggings and soaked underwear before straightening. The buzzing stops in my ass as I do, and a sigh of relief escapes my mouth. Jace continues to stare at me for a moment before he makes a twirling motion with his fingers.

"Spin for me."

I swallow, a blush returning to my cheeks. Being naked is one thing, but spinning around like a ballerina *while* naked?

A playful grin morphs on Jace's lips. "Do I need to ask again, beautiful?"

His words wash over me, reminding me that I'm a confident and desirable woman. I don't need to be self-conscious here. Especially with these two men who have done nothing but make me feel wanted in the short time since we met. I start to spin, making sure to keep my chest and butt out so he has a nice view.

"I see you got your hands on her ass, huh, baby?" he questions Lucas.

A word that sounds like "yes" comes out around Jace's cock as I return to facing forward. My butt must still be red from his spanking in the shower. I guess I didn't realize he'd hit me that hard. All I knew was that it felt wonderful and I liked it.

"You have two choices," Jace says to me. "You can come and help pretty boy here suck my cock, or you can get on your back and suck his dick since he's been such a good boy. Either choice will get you an orgasm, but only if you decide in the next five seconds."

His words hit me, and my heart jumps in my chests. I blink at him in shock, but then he starts counting down like a New Year's Eve clock. "Five, four..."

My brain bounces between options. Sucking Jace's cock with Lucas sounds fun, but I've also been wanting to get my mouth on Lucas's since he got me off in the shower.

"Three, two..."

A squeak leaves my mouth as I make my decision. Before he can get to one, I move behind Lucas's kneeling form and put my hands on the band of his sweats.

Jace makes a sound of approval. "I see our little slut agrees, baby. You've been a good boy so now you get those puffy lips around your cock first. Thank me."

The sound of Lucas popping off Jace's cock sends a jolt through me. "Thank you, Daddy."

"Good boy," he says, wiping a bit of saliva from the corner of Lucas's mouth. "Now keep that mouth full of cock and don't come up for air until our girl gets you off." Lucas keens, going back to his job like the good boy Jace claims him to be.

Holy. Wow. I'm in a dirty fantasyland, and I'm still trying to figure out how the hell I got here when I was supposed to be on a plane to my family right now. When I find Jace's eyes, he smirks at me like he knows what I'm thinking.

"What are you waiting for, beautiful? Take Lucas's dick out and get to work."

I lick my lips and pull on the band of Lucas's sweats to reveal his perfect toned ass that has me salivating to take a bite. I move quicker, wanting to see more of his body again. It's a little difficult to remove his pants with him kneeling, but he helps me as much as he can considering he's got his mouth full of cock. Once they're taken care of, I memorize the picture in front of me.

Jace's still mostly clothed form is resting back against the lounge as Lucas's half clothed body moves, his hands clenching on Jace's tattooed thighs as he works to keep himself kneeling. I wish I could take a picture and use this as "spank bank" material. Not that I've ever had one before, but now I want one just of this night.

Jace clears his throat, and I smile at him sheepishly before I hop into action. I get on to my back and maneuver myself under Lucas. The leather of the couch feels sticky against my overheated skin as I get into position. It's a little tricky and kind of a tight fit, but I can make it work.

With Lucas's sex now above my face, my stomach flutters. I knew he was big, but seeing it this close, it can rival Jace's. But while Jace is wide, Lucas is longer, however they're both perfect and beautiful. They're definitely going to spoil me for all other men going forward.

"Put your hips down a bit, baby. Don't make our little slut work too hard...*yet*," Jace directs Lucas. His vocal teasing has my clit throbbing and I press my thighs together to try and relieve some of the tension.

Jace opens his legs a bit more so Lucas can spread himself wider and not fall, then he dips his hips down so his cock is closer to me. There's a decent amount of pre-cum leaking from the tip, enough that a drop of it lands on my lips. My tongue darts out to taste it, the salty bitter flavor hitting me. My mouth waters as I move myself up enough to take the head of him between my lips. Lucas's body shudders at my touch, his cock twitching. The noise he makes around Jace's cock spurs me on as I take more of him into my mouth. He's heavy and warm, the musk of him filling my senses. I like the feel of the ridges and silky skin against my tongue.

"Does her mouth feel good around your cock, baby?" Jace asks Lucas.

A muffled "yes, Daddy" leaves his lips as I bring one of my hands up to cup Lucas's balls. They tighten in my grip and I suck on the tip of his cock like a lollipop. He lets out a sexy moan that encourages me to take him deeper so he's almost touching the back of my throat. It doesn't get past me that there is, in fact, still half of his cock left. That means he'll probably turn me out while fucking me. I rub my thighs together again but it gives me no relief.

"Our girl is horny," Jace taunts. "She's rubbing her thighs together like the needy slut she is."

I mewl around Lucas's cock; his dirty words make my skin tingle.

"I bet she's soaking the couch right now, baby. Turning it into our own personal Slip 'N Slide."

Lucas's hips punch forward, and his silken head hits the back of my throat. I gag a bit at the sudden intrusion, saliva filling my mouth. But instead of turning me off, I want him to do it again. I thread my arms up so that my hands are now digging into the taut flesh of his ass, taking him deeper into my mouth so I gag again.

"That's it, beautiful. You're doing so well. Suck his cock like you mean it," Jace croons.

I flatten my tongue and take more of him in, sucking and squeezing his ass beneath my palms.

Jace turns his flattery to Lucas. "Watching you take my dick never gets old, baby. You're so good at it." Lucas makes a garbled noise. "That's it, suck harder. You too, beautiful," he says to me.

I smile and do as he asks. Lucas releases a pleasurable cry as I dig my nails into his skin so I'm sure I've left a mark of my own.

"That's it, my pretty little sluts doing exactly as I say." Jace sighs heatedly.

I want to bring my hand down and touch myself so badly, but I'm pretty sure that's against the rules? Is there rules? I have no idea, but by how Jace has been so far, I think I do what he says at this point, which makes my skin even hotter.

"Riley?" Jace asks. "You okay if our pretty boy fucks your face?"

I stop my sucking. *Our* pretty boy. He called me "our girl" earlier, too. The memory has me shivering. His words and the image of Lucas using my mouth like that has a new wave of arousal messing up the expensive couch.

"Yes, I want it," I exhale. "God, I want that so badly."

"Hmm, so dirty." Jace chuckles. "Keep your hands on that nice, pretty boy ass, and if you need to stop, tap him three times with both your hands, got it?"

"Yes, Daddy."

"How many times?"

"Three."

"Good girl. Now open that mouth, and let's see how much you love cock."

Chapter Twelve

Leo

HER MOUTH OPENS WIDE for me, and there's nothing else I can do but sink inside. Those lips were heaven to kiss—but around my cock? Fucking paradise. I groan around Jace's steel length as her tongue slides around my shaft.

When Jace tugs at my hair, I meet his gaze with my mouth still doing its job. He looks back with lust, and there's a bead of sweat forming on his brow. I know he's using everything he has not to blow his load, but he's good at holding himself off for long periods of time. A special talent of his.

"Take care of our girl," he mutters. *Our girl.* I'm not sure if Riley noticed, but he said that earlier too. I wonder if he realizes exactly what he's saying. The endearment has a nice ring to it. It also makes a warm sensation pool in my stomach. I nod to let him know I've heard him loud and clear before I thrust my hips forward and further into Riley's wet mouth. The movement causes her to gag again as I hit the back of her throat, which only makes me want to sink deeper inside.

"Relax and breathe through your nose, Riley." Jace reminds her, both of his hands coming to grip my skull. Oh, shit. He's going face fuck me while I face fuck her. He's a fucking deviant. "That goes for you too, pretty boy."

He shoves my head down his cock without another warning. Now I'm struggling for air and gripping his thighs for reprieve. His length is so thick, so broad, I have to be relaxed to take him down or I'll gag. My jaw is sore already from him using me, but he knows I love it or he wouldn't have me do it.

Riley's nails dig into my ass. I squeeze my eyes shut at the sensation of it all. Her throat constricting tightly around the head of my dick along with Jace's strong hands on my head. It's wonderful, kind of frightening, and also degrading at the same time. I'm so hard that I know I won't last very long, which is exactly what Jace wants. For me to lose control.

Thrusting my hips forward, I start with a slow and deep rhythm to get Riley used to taking my dick in this way. She's a natural, or maybe she's done this before with her stupid ex or another guy. But regardless, I feel comfortable enough to start picking up my pace since she hasn't given any signs she wants to tap out.

"That's it, baby." Jace pulls my hair. "Feed your dick to her sweet mouth, get yourself off. I want you to come down her throat while I come down yours."

My cock pulses as my balls hit Riley's chin amid wet sucking noises. Fuck, she took me all the way down. I knew she could fucking do it. She was made for me in every way possible. I wish I could move my head to see her take me, but Jace would punish the fuck out of me. Which on another day I'd love, but I'm anxious to hear Riley's cries while we screw her brains out.

Jace curls his nails into my scalp at the same time Riley digs hers into my ass even harder that I think I might bleed. My eyes water from the strength of Jace's grip as he pushes me down so my nose is pressed into his pubic bone, and I struggle for air. My hips punch forward and Riley squeezes me harder, sucking me like a champ. Jace moves one of his hands to grip my jaw, pressing my cheeks against his dick and smirking at me like an asshole.

"Make him come, beautiful," he commands Riley. He lets me up off his cock and I suck in a breath through my nose. Drool drips from the side of my lips, then he goes back to furiously fucking my face like I'm just a toy. My watery eyes stay on his handsome face as he smiles adoringly at me.

"Such a good boy," he purrs. "You love my cock, don't you?" Since my mouth is full, I simply nod and make a noise of agreement. I press the pads of my fingers into Jace's thighs as my orgasm rolls closer and my hips move quicker. Riley moans around my cock, and then one of her fingers rim my ass. My orgasm explodes before I can stop it or warn the amazing woman who has my cock stuffed down her throat.

I jerk and come hard, Jace holds my face on his cock as Riley swallows my release, the back of her throat working against my sensitive head. Swear words try to leave my mouth but Jace doesn't let up, he fucks me with wild abandon and I take it because I love it just as much as him.

His body tightens and a throaty moan bubbles from his lips. I hollow my cheeks and push my hands up his thick quads till I'm touching the sensitive flesh of his hips. Within a few seconds he's letting go, his salty come coating the back of my throat as I work it down. I can feel his cock pulsing as he continues to empty himself, his orgasm dragging out as I milk him dry.

When he's finished, Jace lets go of my head and I slowly let his softening length slip from my lips. Not forgetting about Riley, I bring my hips up so I can peak down at her. Her semi-dry strawberry locks are mussed and her cheeks are red from the fucking she just went through. She's also got some mascara that she put on before dinner smudged around her eyes from the tears that welled up. She looks like a sexy vixen, but I can tell she's a lot wound up and a little in shock at what just happened. I make eye contact with Jace, and a silent conversation is had between us.

Jace helps me get off the lounge and I massage my tender jaw before grinning down at Riley. I allow myself a moment to admire her naked form splayed out for us like a sacrifice.

"You okay, Shortcake?" I ask her.

She nods, still in a daze. I remember the feeling of doing an act so dirty you're wondering if maybe something is wrong with you, or if maybe the angels will smite you.

"Pull her up, J," I say.

Jace does what I ask, leaning down to loop his arms under Riley's armpits until he can pull her up like she weighs nothing. Riley squeals as he does it, a sexy noise escaping her lips when she feels his flaccid dick settle between the round globes of her ass, her back now plastered to his chest.

Jace's shining eyes find mine and he dips his head at me in almost a submissive way. I've lost control, and now I'm ready to get lost in the moment. No 'Daddy's or 'Sir's.' I want Riley wild and wanting as I get a taste of that sweet pussy again. If Jace is lucky, I'll even share.

Riley watches me curiously beneath hooded eyes, the multi-colored holiday lights casting a glow on her pale skin. It gives me a devious idea.

"Get Riley all riled up again, would you J?"

He chuffs. "She's already riled up." He brushes a rough hand down her cheek. "Aren't you, beautiful?" He clicks the power on her butt plug again, and the poor thing nearly jumps off the couch.

She whines. "Are you trying to kill me?"

"La petite mort, as the French like to say. So yes?" he teases, sliding his hand from her jaw to her neck. His large palm engulfs the column, squeezing just hard enough to make her moan.

"*Fuckkkk...*" She pushes her ass back onto his cock and writhes around as if she's on fire.

I know she needs to come, and she will. But I want to get her nice and primed for the stuffing she'll soon be getting. I make my way toward the fireplace mantel and see the item I want. When I first saw this specific piece of decor, I told Jace that they looked like dildos or butt plugs. He laughed at the time, but this idea has been rolling around in my head like the dirty perv that I am. But instead of Jace being my plaything, Riley gets the honor.

After I take my time selecting the one I want, I turn back to the sexy lovebirds on my couch. Jace has removed all of his clothing like some ninja, revealing all of his softness and intricate body art on his brown skin. The picture they make together is erotic. Like "Paint me like one of your French girls, Jack" erotic.

Jace has her pinned to him, his legs wrapped around hers to keep her from squirming. It also forces her into a spread-eagle position so her glistening sex is on display. He has his hand back on her throat, gripping softly while his other hand trails in a feather-like movement down her collar bone, through the valley of her breasts and then eventually over each pert nipple. Just as Riley relaxes into him, he brings his hand down to smack one breast, then the other. Our dirty girl releases a string of expletives, but Jace's grip is strong enough that she can't move much.

I grin. "Looks like you got her riled up."

"Are you going to join us or just watch?" He muses.

I growl, removing my shirt and striding over so I can position myself right between their open legs. "No watching for me. Now I get to play." I hold up the smooth, solid glass Christmas tree ornament so they both can see what I have. Riley's head shoots up with Jace's hand still around her neck.

"What are you going to do with that?" she asks, her doe eyes wide.

With an innocent smile I run the rounded tip of the cool glass on her inner thigh, causing her to shiver.

"I'm going to make you feel good, Shortcake."

"But it's for decoration."

"Then you're my tree," I retort.

Jace's warm laugh rumbles through the room, and I'm positive Riley's eyes are trying to escape her skull.

"Just relax, Riley," Jace soothes.

"That's not meant to be inside people. Haven't you ever watched those shows where the ER doctors remove weird items from people's butts?"

We can't help it; both Jace and I start rolling with laughter. Riley stills as we unravel, our cackles coming in waves until we're finally able to catch our breath. She glares at us but in a playful way.

"This isn't going up your ass, Riley. And I promise, it's solid. It's not going to break." I take a few seconds to kiss up her calf until I reach the inside of her knee. Then I trace the glass on her belly, pressing a bit more firmly so she can see it's not flimsy nor sharp in any way.

"I'll take good care of you," I swear.

"We both will," Jace adds.

Her gaze penetrates me, as if she's searching for a lie. But finally, she nods her acquiescence.

"Good." I land an open-mouthed kiss on her thigh. "Now relax, because we're gonna make our good girl come. Aren't we, J?"

He hums in response, his lips landing on the skin of her shoulder as he cups both of her breasts, rolling them in his palms.

"Should I not call you Daddy?" she pants.

"Only if you both want," Jace answers, landing more kisses on her bare skin.

Riley watches me through hooded eyes, my cock aching when I truly take in the view of her spread out by Jace from this angle.

"I want you to scream our names this time, Riley," I say. Then I bury my mouth in her pussy and suck deeply on her clit while Jace pinches both of her nipples.

"Oh my god!" she keens, back bowing. I think someone is still sensitive from earlier.

With a smile on my face, I suck again, using my tongue to lap at her folds. The flavor of her coats my taste buds, and once again, I'm in pussy heaven. With the feeling of the plug buzzing in her ass, I can't help but imagine how that hole will feel all warmed up around Jace's cock. He's going to never want to leave it. *Fuck*. My hips thrust against the couch like some horny teenager as I try to relieve the growing ache in my cock.

"Do you like his face in your cunt, Riley?" Jace asks.

"Yes. God yes," she moans.

"He sucks so good, doesn't he, beautiful?"

"Yes! He's so good at eating my pussy."

I suction her clit harder at the praise, slipping my fingers inside her tight, wet hole. I curl my fingers once I'm all the way in, stroking the delicious G-spot that has her panting. She squirms against Jace's hold, as if the sensation is too much, but his strong body keeps her in place.

I lift my gaze to his while keeping my mouth on Riley. His eyes are lit with a fire I can only describe as utter need. I know what he wants, and since I'm in a sharing mood, I pull my fingers from her wetness and prop myself up enough so that I can bring my fingers to Jace's mouth. Riley observes with interest as he leans his head forward and wraps his lips around my fingers. He pulls them in so his lips hit my knuckles then sucks on them like they're her pussy. Once he's cleaned up every drop, he pulls back and smacks his lips.

"Tastes like shortcake."

Riley whimpers, and the guttural sound that comes out of me almost doesn't sound human. Ravenous, I settle back between her thighs, this time with the ornament at the ready. They watch as I bring the rounded tip to her sex, tracing the cold glass over her heated folds. Riley's body shutters, her head falling back against Jace's chest. He strokes her shoulders and her breasts in soothing manner, whispering something to her I can't hear. Whatever it is relaxes her, and I take the moment to glide the tip of ornament inside her.

She gasps at the feeling. While the object isn't nearly the size of my cock, or Jace's, she's so goddamn tight and responsive that she arches off the cushion. I push the decorative glass tree in, watching as it disappears further inside her body. The sound of her sexy moans cut off as Jace seals his pouty lips over hers, his mouth devouring her. I can almost feel what it's like to have his beard tickling my skin as he kisses me. The sensory memory has me lapping at her cunt again, pushing the thickest part of the ornament in so all that's left is the square base I'm holding on to.

My lips wrap around her clit and I don't hold back as I start to fuck her with the object, enjoying the wet noises it makes and Riley's mewls against Jace's lips. Fuck. I really do come up with the craziest ideas. But this is by far one of my best.

CHAPTER THIRTEEN

Riley

THERE'S A CHRISTMAS ORNAMENT in my pussy and a buzzing butt plug in my ass. Oh, and did I mention there's one hottie eating me out while the other one sucks my face off? Best. Christmas. Ever.

Jace draws me away from my internal fist pump by using his tongue to fuck my mouth almost as deep as Lucas fucked it with his cock. He tastes different from Lucas, like a midnight snowfall mixed with a hint of the herbs from dinner. I love the way his facial hair lightly scratches my skin and his hands feel rough against my breasts. So different from the soft skin of Lucas's hands, which now that I think of it, is strange for a hockey player. Shouldn't they be calloused? But I guess they wear gloves.

Lucas's tongue flicks my clit faster, and I'm no longer thinking about his hands. I fidget and try to close my legs from the onslaught of sensation, but Jace keeps holding me firm so I'm vulnerable to the man who's 'decking the halls,' so to speak.

"You sensitive, beautiful?" Jace asks, his lips trailing kisses down my neck.

"Yes," I answer breathlessly. He sucks on my skin, his fingers rolling my nipples as Lucas eats me like a starved man and fucks me with the ornament. Jesus, this is so dirty. If I was on Santa's nice list before, I'm not now.

Jace presses his mouth to my ear. "How does it feel to have our pretty boy sucking you like he wants to live inside your cunt?"

I let out a desperate, needy, sound at his words. "It feels...it feels..." Lucas nibbles my clit and I cry out, "euphoric!"

Jace growls softly against my skin and then slaps my breasts again out of nowhere. The slight sting along with the pressure of the objects inside me has me teetering on the edge of orgasm.

"She's close, J baby," Lucas says against my clit. He sweeps his tongue over my folds, and two of his fingers probe at my entrance near the ornament. I wail desperately as he slides them in alongside the decoration.

"Does that feel good, Riley?" Jace asks, his breath tickling me.

I nod furiously. "I feel full, like I'm about to—" The words die on my lips as Lucas fucks me faster with the ornament and adds a third finger. The pressure against my G-spot is unlike anything I've felt before. Panic sets in, and I wonder if I'm about to relieve myself. The sensation is heavy and burns a little; it's not unpleasant but it's overwhelming.

Jace holds me, his hand firm against the base of my neck and legs pinning me open. The pressure on my neck is just enough that I lose a little air. It only adds to what's happening in my body. My legs start shaking as Lucas moves faster and faster.

"Oh shit! I can't. I'm gonna—I don't know!" I cry.

"Just let it happen," Jace's deep voice soothes.

I try to do as he says as the pressure inside me continues to build and build. Jace cuts off just a bit more of my air as Lucas suctions my clit hard, pressing a hand against the buzzing plug in my ass. From that point on I become a mess of sensations. Wetness releases from my body and I'm shaking all over while Lucas finger fucks me through the best orgasm of my life.

"That's it, beautiful. Such a good girl," Jace praises, the vibrations of his voice only adding to my pleasure.

My eyes start to roll into the back of my head and I wonder if I'm about to pass out. I can feel Jace rubbing his hands all over my body in a soothing motion while Lucas finally stops his onslaught on my ravaged pussy. After a few seconds, the buzzing in my ass ceases, and Lucas removes the ornament before kissing each of my thighs.

"You okay?" Jace asks, his hand threading through my sweaty hair.

I crack open my eyes and stare into his lovely hazel ones. "I think I died. Did I?"

"No Riley, you didn't die." He chuckles. "You squirted."

CHAPTER FOURTEEN

Jace

RILEY REMINDS ME OF a fish out of water. Her lips are puckered, chest heaving, and her skin is flushed from sex and embarrassment. It's cute, but wholly unnecessary.

"I what now?" She gapes.

"Squirted. All over Lucas's face and couch."

She tries to hide her face, but I stop her, holding her hands in mine. "It was hot, Riley. I don't think I've ever seen a woman come so hard. Have you, baby?" I ask Leo.

He shakes his head, starting to wipe the wetness off his face but I stop him. "Don't wipe away my dessert. Gimme," I say playfully.

Leo stands, his hard dick bobbing against his tight lower abs. He takes the spot on the couch next to me and leans in so our shoulders touch. With Riley safely propped up on my chest, I use one of my hands to grab Leo's slick jaw and lick up the side of his face. Riley shifts her plush ass on my erection and exhales a sexy whimper, watching me as I work my way around his lips, lapping up the tangy flavor before sealing my mouth over his. Pre-cum leaks from my dick, and now all I want is to be inside her tight ass, feeling Leo's cock moving against mine as we kiss and bring our girl to another plane of existence all together.

Leo grabs the back of my head to bring me closer. There's nothing sweet about this kiss. It's full of desire and pure want. Most of our kisses—okay, all of our kisses—are like this, but this one feels particularly charged with Riley here and her scent intermingling with ours. I don't know if Leo has noticed that her presence has already shifted something between us, but there's a difference in the way he's been tonight. He's letting himself be freer.

With his brother's career skyrocketing to the stratosphere lately, I know he's been overworked and overwhelmed, which is one of the many reasons I took charge to get things started. He does better when he has a balance, but he won't listen to anyone about taking a break—not even me. I think that's why he doesn't get in the Christmas spirit either; people like to go visit their family and take a breather. But I know when he goes home to Seattle, Lucas and his family talk about hockey. Even his relatives just ask him about Lucas, never about his business or what he's built from the ground up with me by his side.

Dread fills my chest at what's going to happen when he finally tells Riley who he is. I know she isn't going to be happy about it, and she'll be angry at me, too. Our little bubble will burst, and this insanely perfect woman will probably walk out the door and never speak to us again. Just like Leo, I thought it would be sex, and that's it, which is why I ultimately went along with it. But now I get the feeling it won't be that simple.

Leo bites my lip and tugs on it. I focus on the man I love kissing the hell out of me, and the woman who's randomly turned my world upside down, gripping my thighs with her hands and rubbing on my dick like it's a genie lamp.

"You taste so good on pretty boy's lips, Shortcake," I say, pulling back to lick a drip of sweat off Leo's cheekbone.

Leo runs his hands down my chest. "It's the perfect nickname, isn't it?"

"You did good, baby," I boast.

He smiles his one-dimpled smile that does something to my insides. Fuck me sideways. Why am I acting like he's my partner? I mean he is, and we both love each other, but he's not my monogamous boyfriend or husband. We made it clear to Riley earlier what we are to each other, and it's been good enough for the last few years. So why do I feel like I need more now?

Leo kisses me again before working his way down my neck, moving his body so he can get to Riley. Her rounded cheeks look like Pink Lady apples and her eyes are glassy post-orgasm. She smiles adoringly at him once his face is near hers. He returns it, then lovingly tucks a loose strand of hair behind her ear. A sharp sensation shoots through my heart that almost has me reaching up to rub my chest. It's not jealousy, but a foreign feeling. Fulfillment, maybe? Rightness?

This voluptuous, strawberry-blonde, snowstorm of a woman came into our lives only hours ago, yet somehow she's done something I haven't been able to do for Leo in the last few years. She's softening him. He hasn't acted this lovey-dovey or called me so many pet names since the early days of us fucking. But was it ever only "fucking" with us?

Leo must sense my overthinking because he brings his hand up to tug on my head. "I want to try something."

I quirk an eyebrow at him as he maneuvers Riley until he has her where he wants her. With a hand now on the back of her head, and a hand on mine, he pulls us together and kisses her, then me. Soon, there's tongues and teeth and limbs everywhere as we sloppily do some odd three-way kiss. It's messy, and this chaise lounge isn't the best for this move—but somehow, it works.

After a minute, I pull back on Leo's lip and bite it hard enough that he hisses.

"Let's move this party to the bedroom, or we'll end up on the floor," I say. "Your leather couch may be water-resistant, but your fancy carpet isn't."

Riley flushes from the memory of her squirting, and I give her a simple kiss.

"We want you to come like a waterfall, beautiful. Let's just avoid having to pay for pretty boy's new carpet."

She swats my chest, making Leo laugh. I know he doesn't care about the carpet, but I want the large space of the bed for what's about to happen next.

Leo stands up and holds out a hand to Riley. He looks hot, bathed in the colored lights of the room. I'm regretting not fucking him in here before. I guess there's still after Christmas if he doesn't go to Seattle tomorrow, or if we leave up the decor after New Year's.

Once Riley is up, she holds out her hand to me. The gesture only makes me want to keep her more. She's thoughtful and getting comfortable enough now that I don't think she even remembers we're naked—or that she still has a butt plug in her ass.

Leo tugs us forward, and we all move linked together through the space until we're in Leo's master bedroom. He turns on the lights so there's just enough for us to see the room and its blue-toned decor. This room is probably one of my favorites in the house. It's spacious and decorated just enough that it feels comfortable without feeling too sparse or cluttered.

"Holy cow! Your place keeps getting better and better," Riley exclaims.

Leo drops her hand and moves to the gas fireplace, flipping it on so there's a nice glow in the room.

"Is that a California King?!" she squeals.

"You bet," Leo says.

I use her moment of stunned astonishment to start pushing her back until her legs hit said California King. She laughs as she falls on the soft mattress, her lovely body bouncing as I prowl over her. The sound of her giggles cease as my lips find hers again.

I love the way her large tits push into my chest and our stomachs seem to mold together. I've always preferred women who were built like me, ones I can grab on to and toss around. Ones that I can lay my full body weight on and know I'm not going to crush them. It's one of the reasons why I love men, too. The hardness, the strength; it's unmatched.

Speaking of, I reach my hand out to Leo, keeping my mouth on Riley's as I kiss her like she's the air I need to breathe. His hand entwines with mine, and that pain returns to my chest, like someone is squeezing my heart. I grip his hand, then pull him toward us. He lands on the bed beside Riley, and I move my lips to his. I love how different it feels kissing them both. While Riley is pliant and warm, Leo is all angles and muscles.

Without being prompted, Riley maneuvers herself out from under me, and I take the hint at what she wants. I prowl over Leo and kiss him deeper while Riley trails her hand down my back, then squeezes my ass. My dick swells against Leo's, and we both let out a shuttering groan.

"May I?" Riley asks in her musical voice. She's gesturing to our cocks pressed together. They're both hardening again, but could use a little love.

I grin. "You never have to ask to play with our cocks, beautiful."

Even in the dim room, I can see her flush, but that doesn't stop her from moving so she can access what she's asked for. Leo and I watch as she brings her hand up to her mouth then spits into her palm. The action is almost too dirty coming from her, but she was also choking on Leo's dick not too long ago.

"Goddamn, Shortcake," Leo says with a groan. "You sure are a surprise."

The corners of her lips turn up as she spits into her other hand, then wraps them around both our cocks, rubbing Leo's with mine. I let out a string of curses at the added friction, pressing my forehead into his.

"Kiss each other," she commands us softly.

A needy whine escapes Leo's mouth at her words. "Fuck. She's going to kill me."

A smile plays at my lips. It shouldn't surprise me that Riley's asking for what she wants in this way, but at the same time, I knew she had it in her. She just needed to feel safe to explore all sides of herself. So I do as she asks, my lips descending on Leo's to obey her.

He opens for me with no hesitation, our tongues dancing together in an intoxicating push and pull for dominance. Riley continues to jerk us off together, her soft sounds of excitement only adding to the heated moment. When her hands pull away and she moves, Leo mumbles something against my lips about how much I'll love her mouth. It isn't until Riley's lips are sealed over the crown of my length that I know why he said it.

"Oh fuck!"

She sucks me further in, Leo kissing my bearded jaw. "She's amazing, isn't she?" he says in wonder.

I nod my head, seeking his kiss out again as Riley licks her tongue across my slit like she's savoring her favorite ice cream. She moans at the taste, pulling back to rub Leo and me together again with more vigor.

"You're both so different," she appraises. "Both so big, so perfect. I want to bring your dicks home with me when I leave."

I drop my head to Leo's shoulders and chuckle.

"Maybe I'll have two molds made for you, Shortcake." Leo eyes shine as he says it, looking down to watch as she continues to give us the most amazing handy of our lives. I know I can speak for Leo in this case, too.

Riley pouts. "Not the same."

Leo taps my shoulder and motions his head for me to move. Then, with a quickness only he can have, he pulls a squealing Riley up so she's in the space he's created between us. Her laughter quickly dies when he places his hand on her throat, moving to hover over her so he looks deeply into her eyes.

"Then we better fuck you so good you'll never forget what they feel like."

"Is that a promise?" she asks breathlessly.

He growls. "It's a fact." He kisses her hard, gripping her throat as she opens her mouth to him. Riley meets him stroke for stroke, not backing down, their lips seeking and devouring each other.

I roll to the bedside table to grab lube and condoms while they're swept up in each other, then settle back in to watch some more. If we can convince Riley to share a bed with us again, I'd love to watch her and Leo play together, preferably in a whole scene. They're both so fucking sexy, and the yin and yang of their bodies makes my cock as hard as a rock. I sweep my hand down Leo's back, relishing in the feel of his toned body that he works so hard to have.

While he doesn't play hockey anymore, the man keeps himself in shape like he's in the NHL alongside Lucas. I asked him once why he put so much pressure on himself to look this way, but he just waved me off. It was clear by his reaction he didn't want to talk about it, so I never forced him on the subject. Though my guess is the exact reason why he just didn't come clean to Riley before she came home with us: there's a part of him that feels less than Lucas, so he always has to keep up. And tonight, he wanted to be the person Riley thinks he is because in his mind, even if he'll never admit it, he thinks she'd be disappointed. Which is why I've let it slide this long, although it's bullshit.

Riley's hand reaches for me, and I lock our fingers together. She breaks Leo's kiss, then tugs me so we're kissing again. I let myself get caught up in her; her scent, her taste, how her delicate lips feel so different than the man I've come to love and need so desperately in my life, even when he's being an idiot. When Leo's hand pumps my dick, I let out a feral noise and end the kiss.

"I need you both right fucking now," I express. My voice sounds not like my own. Instead, it's the voice of a man consumed by undeniable want. I blindly pat my hand on the bed until I have two condoms in my hand.

When I hold out one to Leo, he shakes his head. My forehead shoots up. Leo always uses a condom unless it's just us. The last thing he's ever wanted is for one of the women he's slept with to show up on his doorstep pregnant or with a long-lost baby.

"I want to feel you both, no barriers," he says passionately. He stares into Riley's eyes. "I want to watch our come spill out of you, then lick it clean."

"Fucking hell, baby," I sputter. He knows I have a breeding kink, and the image has the base of my spine tingling and my hips thrusting. "You're sure?" I ask him.

"Very sure."

"Riley?"

She nods her head. "I'm on the pill and," she says the next part shyly, "I want to feel you both. I've never felt, I want to—"

I kiss her lips to shut her up, then make a show of tossing the condoms on the ground. My heated gaze finds Leo's. "I get dibs on her ass first."

He smirks. "It's all yours, J baby."

CHAPTER FIFTEEN

Leo

I TAKE THE LEAD, helping Riley move up the bed so she's propped on the pillows. She looks fucking sexy, her voluptuous body a pretty contrast against my rumpled blue comforter and white pillows. Before she can breathe, Jace gets to work between her legs closing his mouth over the hard nub between her folds.

She cries out, her clit sensitive from the first two orgasms I gave her. But for what she's about to experience, we want her to be as wet as possible. While Jace eats her out, finally tasting her sweetness from the source, I move behind him so I can have a little fun before the party officially starts. I get to my knees and spread his ass cheeks wide, revealing the rosebud I want to tease. It pulses a bit in anticipation, then I dive in. I use my tongue to rim him, dipping in and out as he curses into Riley's pussy. He loves when I eat his ass, and the noises he makes are always out of this world.

He pushes his ass back, allowing me to pull his cheeks wider so I can get better access. From this point of view, I can see Riley gripping Jace's tousled hair, crushing his willing mouth into her cunt as he tries to suffocate me with his ass. The sinful sight has my cock so painfully hard that it reminds me of the ornament I worked up Riley's wet hole earlier. The need to be inside my pretty Shortcake while Jace has his way with her is almost unbearable. My skin is hot and itchy, and I thrust my hips against the bed to get some sort of relief. After another few dips of my tongue and a smack on his ass, I decide I can't contain myself any longer. I crawl so I'm next to Riley, the heat of her pleasured body searing my skin.

"Get over here, Riley. I want your perfect cunt all over my dick."

She flashes those stunning pine eyes at me, a slow smile inching on her lips as she removes her hands from Jace's head. Jace doesn't bother wiping the shine from his face as he wordlessly helps her straddle my narrow hips that I've propped up with a pillow. When the outer lips of her slick pussy connect with the hard length of me, I let out an almost painful hiss, my eyes rolling back. My aching desire to be inside her only intensifies as she presses her hands to my chest so she can move her needy slit over me in a steady cadence.

I grip my hands on the bold flesh of her waist. "Goddamn, Shortcake. Your pussy is burning me alive and I'm not even inside you yet."

She whimpers. "I need to feel you fuck me. Please, I can't wait anymore."

"Get her on my cock, Jace."

He doesn't need to be told twice. Riley lifts her ass up a bit so Jace can free my leaking cock, his large hand wrapping around my Riley-soaked shaft as he pumps me a few times.

I glare at him, my tone scolding. "Don't tease me, J."

He fucking winks at me and gives my hard flesh one more tug for good measure before placing me at Riley's entrance.

"Sink down, beautiful," he coaches her.

"But the plug..."

He gives her a reassuring smile. "You'll be fine, I promise. Your body is ready for us."

After a moment, she exhales shakily and nods, using her hands on my chest to leverage her body as she torturously begins to lower herself on my length.

"Oh shit, oh shit," she cries, her eyes squeezing shut. "Oh god, baby."

Baby. I like the way she says it. The tone is delicate compared to how Jace says it, but it has my poor cock threatening to spill just the same. *Fuck.* I'm screwed. With everything I have, I pull my focus back to the goddess on top of me and force myself to not lose it.

"Just breathe, Riley," I soothe. "You're opening up so nicely for me."

She whimpers again and Jace takes it as a cue to step in. He moves one of his hands to grasp her head while keeping his other on the base of my cock. He crushes his lips to hers, practically sucking the air from her lungs as a distraction. With his magical lips attached to hers, she lowers herself down inch-by-inch, her nails digging harder into my pecs the further she goes. It feels like heaven.

Jace removes his hand as she fully seats herself on me, the dimpled skin of her ass pressing down onto my pelvis. I let out a grunt of pleasure as Riley breaks the kiss and moans so loudly that my dick has its own heartbeat now.

"Oh fuck!" we chant together, her body falling forward so her round breasts mold to my chest and her damp forehead presses against mine.

"Such a good girl," I murmur, brushing a lock of hair from her cheek. "You feel like a vice around my cock, Shortcake." She sighs in response. "Let me know when you're ready to move, okay?"

She nods, shifting her hips in small movements until noises that should be illegal spill from her pouty lips. I manage to pry my gaze from her to stare at Jace's hulking nude form, one that I've come to know like the back of my hand. He's still kneeling, his eyes on the space where Riley and I are joined while one hand fists that gorgeous cock of his and the other rests near her waist. The squeeze of Riley's tight cunt while he jacks himself off is almost too much for my brain to handle.

Riley's sex-laden voice thankfully pulls me back to reality. "I'm ready," she says.

I grip her hips to lift her up a bit, one of my hands resting over the one Jace has on her.

"Hold on tight, Shortcake."

Her eyes widen slightly just as I thrust my hips in a short upward motion. The gentle force causes her sharp nipples to rub against my chest in a way that makes my body quake.

"You feel," Riley trails off, her lips brushing against mine, "so good."

Her encouragement makes me punch my hips up harder, both of us crying out at the insane sensation of being joined together with no barriers.

"Your greedy pussy is gripping me so good, Shortcake. Fuck, you're perfect."

She tightens her already snug channel in answer, a fresh wave of her arousal leaking onto my balls. The bed rocks as she picks up speed, pressing herself up so that she can get a better angle to work herself on my cock at a slow pace. Jace's breathing quickens as he strokes himself faster, and a bead of his pre-cum falls on to the comforter. A groan escapes my lips when Riley fucks herself harder on my cock. When I find Jace's blown-out hazel gaze, my chest tightens like a sling shot. His eyes are locked on mine, and within their depths I swear I see a million words unsaid.

It must be the intimacy of the moment, or maybe Riley is a magical unicorn sent to me on Christmas Eve to pull feelings from me that I've long buried—but I'm suddenly overwhelmed with my love for Jace. I think of the moment we met, how he picked me up and dusted me off. How he's held my hand through hard times and had my back when I needed it.

I think of all the nights we've shared and the hours we've talked, and it all feels like too much. Too big. Too...*everything*. He shoots me a warm smile, one that says he knows what I'm feeling, and I swear my heart grows three sizes. I run my tongue along the back of my teeth and try to form words that would be appropriate, but there aren't any.

Tension builds in my chest, so I squeeze my lids shut, willing the emotions inside me to calm. I'm trying too hard to understand why meeting this beautiful woman is what finally made me see that Jace and I should be more than what we are—or if I'm being honest with myself—admit that we already have been more. A lot more.

The bed moves, and the heat of Jace's body sears into me. I don't open my eyes as he tickles my jaw with his nose, his hot breath skittering across my face as he rains kisses all over my face and neck.

"We'll talk later," he whispers. Then he kisses me hard while Riley's moan has me pulling my attention back to the moment. She deserves for me to be all here with her and Jace. And I'm committed to fulfilling all the promises I made her.

"I love watching you two together," Riley says, her cunt squeezing the life out of me. "You're both so handsome, so gentle yet rough and—" I thrust up inside her. "Fuck!" she cries.

"I love watching you ride my cock," I say with a grunt, my tone playful and teasing. "Doesn't she make a perfect slutty cowgirl, J?"

His hungry gaze roves over her body, both of us watching as she throws her head back and bounces on my cock. It's one hell of a sight. Her large breasts swinging, her face riddled with pleasure as she takes what she wants. It's amazing how far she's come since we met in the airport only hours ago. It makes me even harder inside her. She's so fucking good. When one of her hands leaves my chest so she can rub her clit, I know it's time.

"She's ready for you," I tell Jace.

Riley halts her movements, eyes popping open to look at Jace's straining cock.

"Do you really think it will fit?" she asks. Her voice is so goddamn cute I almost lose it again.

"Oh, Shortcake," I say. "If I can take it, so can you."

That needy whine escapes her lips again, and I know she really is ready for it. She's capable of more than she gives herself credit for. I hope that when she leaves here, she feels more confident in herself and what she can do, and how amazing she is.

Jace kneels on the bed so he can kiss her forehead, whispering words of encouragement in her ear before he grabs the bottle of lube.

"Lie on my chest, Riley," I instruct her.

She follows my orders, plastering her breasts to me as I embrace her and move my legs and hips a bit so we're connected in every way possible. Jace positions himself behind her and palms her ass cheeks, running one of his thick fingers down her crack until he reaches the plug. He taps it playfully, and Riley hisses like a cat. It's adorable and sweet that she thinks that will stop him from playing.

"Is your ass ready for my cock, beautiful girl?" He groans, running the broad head of himself up and down her crack.

"Yes, Daddy."

Jace lets out a string of fucks and Riley grins at me. She has Jace figured out already. If he's going to play, she'll play, too.

He smacks her ass, and she moans against my neck.

"Harder, J. She likes it harder."

Riley bites my pec, then cries out as Jace lays down a series of smacks that make her ass jiggle and her pussy clench around my dick so hard that my soul leaves my body.

"Jesus, you're so fucking tight," I say before grabbing her jaw to lay a sloppy kiss on her. She bites my lower lip as Jace spanks her a few more times. When she breaks away, panting, he stops.

"I'm going to pull the plug out now, Riley," he says. "Relax and breathe out when I do, okay?"

She nods, pressing her forehead into the crook of my shoulder. Jace catches my eye as he moves the plug around in her tight hole before slowly pulling it out. Riley cries out, her nails digging into my biceps. I'm sure that was sensitive as fuck, which makes the pounding we're about to give her ten times more likely to have her passing out with pleasure.

I brush some hair from her forehead as Jace squirts a generous amount of lube on his fingers. I bring one of my hands to tilt Riley's face so her pine green eyes are looking into mine.

"It's gonna feel like a lot at first, but don't push him out. Just relax and give into it. I promise you'll be more than okay."

Her face looks a bit nervous, but I can see the excitement shining behind it.

"I'm ready," she says, breathing out.

I glance to Jace who looks as if he's about to combust. He nods and puts the tip of his thick cock at her back entrance. This entire moment reminds me of the first time I bottomed for him. It was a little frightening to be honest, but so euphoric once I let myself take it. Now with Riley, it's like I'm reliving that moment, but it's ten times better because I'm inside her cunt and emotions are involved.

"Take a deep breath in, Riley," Jace tells her gently. As soon as she does, he pushes the tip inside and she squeals.

"You're okay, you're okay," I chant. "You're such a good girl taking his big cock." My words have her moaning, and I pet her hair while making sure to keep still.

She takes another breath, then says, "More, Jace."

He guides himself in an inch more, his body trembling as he holds himself back. "You're so snug, fuck Riley. I'm gonna come in this ass so hard." He grunts, his voice more caveman than ever.

Riley's pussy squeezes me again, and her fresh arousal wets us both. She fucking loves this. I'm already dreaming of all the ways we can fuck her, and we haven't even finished one complete round yet.

"Jace, oh shit!" she cries as he moves further and further in.

"He's halfway in." I groan. "I can feel his cock inside you."

"Halfway?!" she exclaims.

Jace manages a smile as he keeps himself from bottoming out like I know he wants to.

"You take our cocks like they're meant for you, Riley," Jace says, exhaling in pleasure.

I bite the inside of my cheek to try and hold myself together. I've DP'd women many times before this, but the chemistry between the three of us, it sets something off in me, as though I'm a born-again virgin. The sensation of Jace's cock sliding in and in and in—it's an experience I don't think I can even describe.

"I'm so full, I'm—oh God, this is—oh shit!" Riley cries, her voice high-pitched.

I brush the hair from her face and make sure she's breathing. Her eyes are glassy, and for a second I'm worried we're hurting her.

"Are you good, Riley?"

She vigorously shakes her head in a nod. "I'm good, just—" Jace bottoms out and she screams. "Oh fuck, Jace!"

Jace hums in satisfaction and rubs the globes of her ass in appraisal. "You feel so fucking good, Riley. Jesus, you're so perfect."

"You are perfect," I reiterate, kissing her lips as if I'm sipping a fine wine. When I've had my fill, her body relaxes against my chest and she tips her chin down.

"I think I need you both to move now," she says.

Jace and I make eye contact. I signal him to make the first movement. We've been together for so long that our timing is practiced and efficient. If there's something we'd always win first prize at, it's group sex and satisfying our partners. And maybe making our clients millionaires, too.

As he pulls his cock out, then pushes back in, Riley and I let a string of expletives together. The feeling of us all connected, bare and silken, it's...Like I said, I can't describe it. The only thing I can think to say is it's a fucking revelation.

"Lucas," she moans out. "I need, I need..."

I scrunch my forehead together in pain from the name she just called me, but pretend she said Leo instead. "What do you need, Riley?"

"Move, touch me. Oh, fuck, I need something. More, anything!" she wails in heated desperation.

"Your wish is our command." Jace moves out and I move forward, fucking her deep until she screams in pleasure. She bites my chest as I retreat and Jace thrusts back in from behind. We start a slow pace of seesawing back and forth to warm her up before we abandon playing nice. After a moment, I thread my fingers through her hair and force her eyes to mine.

"Can you get on your forearms for me?" I ask. "I want to suck your pretty tits while we fuck you."

She bites her lip and nods her head. When she's in position, I use my hands to grab my desired toys and squeeze them while Jace thrusts back in.

"Yes! Oh, Jace, Lucas, fuck!" she cries. Her face reflects pure ecstasy just as I latch my mouth onto one nipple and suck. Our girl writhes between us as Jace and I start to thrust at the same pace. *Fuck*. Our cocks seem to almost meld together as we fill her to the brim again and again.

"So good, beautiful. You're such a little slut for our cocks, aren't you?" Jace groans.

"Yes! Yes, you both feel so good inside me," she keens.

I suck her nipple harder and she starts to move her hips with us. Like I said before, a natural.

Jace and I moan with her now, the sounds of her wet pussy and the slapping of skin the soundtrack to our Christmas debauchery.

"I've never felt this way before," Riley murmurs, rocking her hips just right so she's hitting her clit against me.

Jace thrusts harder. "Like what, beautiful?"

She expels another loud cry and says, "Like I'm falling and I don't know when or where I'll land."

Jace moves one of his hands and grips a fistful of her hair, pulling back just enough that her back dips and her ass arches into Jace's pelvis. The new angle gives me more room to thrust, and allows Jace more momentum as well.

Riley swears as we drill into her, the new sensation of Jace pulling on her scalp releasing more endorphins into her system. The image of her tits above me and her face strained in pleasure while Jace fucks the life out of her will forever be burned into my memory. Her pussy pulses around my cock, and I know she's close.

"You can fall anytime you want, Shortcake. I promise we'll catch you," I say with conviction.

The green eyes I've come to adore flash open to meet mine, and I think I see tears form in them, but she quickly blinks them away before I can know for sure.

"Come for us, Riley," Jace encourages her now.

His eyes meet mine, and by the tense lines between his brow, I know he's ready to blow his load inside her. Imagining it dripping out of her luscious ass for the rest of the night has me right on the edge, ready to fall.

Riley undulates her hips, and I motion for Jace to bring her forward again. I want her sandwiched between us with his lips on mine while we come together. Jace lets go of her hair and I help ease her down on my chest. Riley trembles in my arms, as if she's about to lose control.

"Spooning," Jace tells me suddenly, pulling his dick out quick enough that she whines from the loss of it.

"We're adjusting, beautiful." He chuckles. "You'll have my cock back in your ass in two seconds." I can't help but laugh, too. Only Jace could make this moment light and fun, while really I feel as if what's happening here is changing everything.

Jace helps adjust us so that Riley and I are on our sides, her ass facing Jace as he spoons her from the right. The moment he's in position he doesn't give her any warning before thrusting his cock back in her willing hole.

"Jace!" Her hips shoot forward so fast that my cock goes deep inside her pussy to the point she screams again.

He sucks on her neck and huffs out a laugh. "You wanted it, beautiful."

She leans her head back against his chest and opens her mouth so that he can slip his tongue inside. I watch them kiss as Jace reaches his arm across Riley until his hand finds mine. We entwine our fingers, sandwiching her between us.

She breaks her lips away. "Harder, God please. Harder."

I smirk at Jace, and we give our little slut what she asks. Our hips move in tandem, our bodies lost in a tangle of limbs and sweat. I don't know what switch flipped—maybe it was the position—but it's like we've become possessed with the need to feel and lose ourselves in each other.

The sound of skin on skin and our moaning fills my ears and my lower belly tenses. Riley's pussy is fluttering, and I know she's close. I free my hand from Jace's and pull her leg over my hip so I can have better access to her clit.

At the touch of my fingers on her wet slit, she purrs with pleasure, her head dropping back against Jace's shoulder as he fucks her harder. Every punch of his hips, he pushes her into me and it feels like heaven and sin all at the same time.

"Oh shit! I'm coming," Riley says, practically weeping.

Jace bites into her shoulder gently as we both thrust harder. The friction of Jace's cock and the sound of Riley's oncoming orgasm has me almost there. I move my leg so that I trap Jace's ankle and prop myself up just enough that he can meet me for a brief kiss. The closeness presses us all together, tightening Riley's holes on our cocks enough for us to all make an unholy noise. I rub her sensitive bud once, then twice, and on the third time, she comes undone in our arms.

"Oh yes, oh God, oh god, yes, yes!"

"That's it, baby. Squeeze our fucking cocks," Jace smoothly commands, his dick still slamming home as he chases his own release.

Riley's fingers grip his beard as she floats into outer space and her inner muscles shake and twitch. I continue to thrum her clit to draw out her orgasm as I piston my hips again and again.

"Fuck, Shortcake. This pussy, this ass, your body, it's fucking ours," I say.

Jace growls his approval as he reaches over to grab my thigh. He digs his short nails into my skin and we lock eyes. As we both pick up our pace, Riley cries out again as another orgasm builds inside her.

"Our little slut is needy for us, baby," Jace says to me.

"Come again, Riley," I demand.

She mewls and shakes her head. "I don't think I can."

"You can, and you will." I rub her clit faster this time and roll my hips, her come coating my fingers as I work her higher and higher.

"Oh for the love of—" she cries.

Jace trails his hand from her breast down between our bodies. Before I see what he's doing, his hand brushes against my cock as it moves in and out of her.

"Fuck, Jace!"

"I'm about to come," he says with a groan. "Both of you, come with me."

He squeezes my balls just as I pinch Riley's clit, and it's all over for us.

I can faintly hear Jace slamming into Riley and the grunt that comes with his release. I think I hoarsely cry both of their names, but I'm too distracted by Riley squirting all over my hand and her pussy milking the come out of my cock.

I don't know how long I empty into her, but my release shoots out in thick jets, coating her insides and leaking out of her pussy. Goddamn, I think I feel Jace's release in her ass. I don't know if that's possible, but I can feel him pulsing and the heat of it on my sensitive shaft.

My head falls to Riley's shoulder where I plant a kiss on her salty skin. Her eyes are closed and her breathing is heavy, matching mine and Jace's. Jace looks just as sated and happy as she does, a look that, now that I think of it, I haven't seen much off late. Fuck, he's beautiful.

When his eyes meet mine, I mouth, "I love you."

His lips turn up, and he mouths it back before blinking down at Riley. She's either floating in orgasmland or is about to fall asleep. That tightness in my chest returns as he brushes a lock of sweat soaked hair from her forehead to press a kiss to it. Riley hums in satisfaction, and then he returns his gaze to mine.

He doesn't have to say what he's thinking, because I already know. He wants Riley just as much as I do. The sex we had only proves that something is going on between us, even if it's ridiculous and unexplainable; especially since we just met her.

I reach over her body to grab his hand and stroke my thumb across his knuckles. He grips my fingers and relaxes against the pillow, his eyes drifting shut. For now, I'm not going to think about what eventually has to be said between us all, including the matter of my real name. For now, reality can go to hell. I'm fine right here with Jace and Riley.

Chapter Sixteen

Riley

I wake up feeling warm. Very warm. My eyes adjust to the dim light of dawn creeping through the bedroom windows, and suddenly the urge to pee becomes overwhelming. When I try to get up, I find I can't. My vision finally focuses to Jace's tattooed arm draped across my middle with Lucas's ankle hooked over mine.

Now I know why I'm so warm. As I test out to see if I can move without waking them, I stifle a groan of pain. My body is wrecked, but in the best way possible. A blush creeps up my cheeks as last night's activities flood back into the forefront of my mind. It's then I realize I don't remember at all what happened after I came for at least the fourth time last night. But I don't feel crusty, which means I had to have been cleaned? Or I just don't remember cleaning myself.

A pink flush covers the rest of my body at the idea of these sexy ass men cleaning me while I was out of it. It's also super sweet and over the top, which aligns with their personalities. My bladder protests again, advising me to get out of bed before I pee myself. I take a deep breath, then gently start to move my ankle out from under Lucas. He doesn't stir at all, then I move on to Jace's arm. It's a bit more difficult to maneuver, but I grab a loose pillow and start to shimmy out as gently as I can. He moves a bit, mumbling something about Santa's cookies before falling asleep again.

I smile to myself at his cuteness. Such a difference from the domineering man last night who called me a slut and had me deep throat cock. My pussy gets wet just thinking about it, and I have the urge to scold it. I'm way too sore and I need to see if I can get on a flight home this morning or I'll miss Christmas with my family altogether.

Once I'm free from the bed, I stare down at my naked body. I have a few fingerprint bruises on my thighs forming, and I'm sure I'll find hickeys on several body parts. But I kind of like it. They marked and owned me. It was the hottest fucking night of my life. I realize my clothes are in the guest room, so I grab a black long-sleeved shirt from a nearby dresser and slip on a pair of giant slippers that I find. Thankfully, the shirt must be Jace's, so I'm able to throw it over my head before seeking out a bathroom. I could go into the master bath, but I don't want to wake the boys. So I make my way through the cold penthouse until I find one closer to the kitchen.

After I relieve myself and wash my hands, I get a good look at my reflection in the mirror. My hair is a rat's nest, and I can see a bit of mascara still on my lashes, but the guys must have cleaned any evidence of the racoon eyes I'm sure I had. There's also a nice hickey on my breast and a bite mark on my ass. I would have thought it would still be red, but there's no evidence of handprints there to tell that story.

But more than the marks, I can't help but be taken with how different I look. It's almost like the pounding they gave me added several years onto my life. My eyes are brighter, my skin is practically glowing, and I feel relaxed. More relaxed than I have been in years. I run my hands over the rolls and curves of my body, loving the way they feel beneath my palms. Chad had beaten me down the last couple years, but this morning, it's like he doesn't even exist. I feel like a queen. A queen who was worshiped by two of the hottest men I've ever seen.

My nipples pebble, and my skin tightens with desire as I think of them lying in bed together. I wonder if we can sneak another round in before we leave. My throbbing pussy disagrees with that idea. Okay, a round of oral. I bet they wouldn't mind one bit if they woke up with my lips and hands on their delicious cocks. I know this was supposed to be a one-night thing, but this morning is okay, right? My stomach flops, and now I don't want this to be just some random night with an airport stranger and his "best friend." I can't help but feel like last night was more than that.

My good mood dissipates as I second-guess what I do or do not mean to the men in the other room. It's silly of me to think this could be more than just a fuck. They said themselves that they don't do commitment, and if they can't even say they're really together even though they love each other, how in the hell would the three of us be in a relationship? I mean, I don't even know how that would work. Could I even be in a poly relationship with two men who care that deeply for one another?

I grip the sink and take a breath to calm my spiraling, as silly as it is. People have one-night stands and kinky sex all the time. *Sigh.* I just can't help but think last night was meant to happen. The deep-seated gut feeling that those men were meant to come into my life. It wasn't just the sex that I enjoyed, it was them. The way they were together, the way they took care of me even after sex, the way they fed me dinner and made sure I was comfortable every step of the way. I mean, I guess they would do that for all their partners, but I was the first they didn't use a condom with...

Am I stupid for thinking that means something?

This is why I never was good at one-night stands. I'm a relationship girl. I get attached and hyperfixate, which is exactly what is happening now. I splash some cool water on my face and take another few deep breaths before I decide it's time to find my phone and get my flights sorted. In the light of day, real life has hit me, and I have to be realistic about what happens from here on out.

I exit the bathroom, glad to find the penthouse still quiet. Eventually, I find my phone on the kitchen island, charging. Tears sting my eyes at yet another thoughtful thing the guys did for me while I was passed out. There are a few text messages from my mom and sister that came in last night. It's just after six in the morning here, which means it's only three in Seattle. They'll be sleeping for at least another four hours. I tap open the one from Mom, and it's just a reminder to let her know what happens with my flights as soon as I hear something. When I read the ones from Stevie, I shake my head.

Stevie: Christmas Eve sucks without you. Dad's making me watch The Christmas Story. You know how much I can't stand Ralphie.

Stevie: Anyway, you're probably sleeping or Chad convinced you to spend Christmas Eve with him. I hope it's the first one. Love you and hope you can get here by tomorrow night so you have to suffer with me.

Stevie is going to freak when I tell her where I spent Christmas. Which reminds me. Lucas and I were going to be on the same flight, so maybe we'll at least have the flight home if we can get there. Though he'll probably be in first class.

I swallow the lump of sadness down and click to my airline app. Looks like I can get on a flight later this afternoon. Which, considering how much snow we had, I'm kind of surprised. But also happy I'll get to dish with Stevie and have a girls' night.

After getting my flight settled, I shoot a text to Mom to let her know that if all goes well, I'll be home for a late dinner or at least dessert. She doesn't answer, but she'll get it as soon as she wakes up, and that's all that matters. I place my phone back on the counter and rub my palms together to warm them up. I guess I'll have a bit of time to kill while they clear the roads. Despite all my fears, I'm glad I get to live out this fantasy a little longer.

With that in mind, I start looking through the cupboards to see what kind of breakfast supplies they have so I can surprise them with a Christmas morning breakfast. After rummaging around for a bit, I manage to find all the ingredients to make pancakes and eggs. I also spot a coffee machine that looks easy enough to use, thank goodness. I was worried he'd have a full Italian coffee bar and I'd have to wait for them to wake up to get my morning fix.

I flip on the machine and find a light for the kitchen. While I wait for my coffee to brew, I take in my surroundings a bit more. Lucas's penthouse looks different in the light of day, especially without the fireplace and the Christmas lights on. Before I start cooking, I decide to check out the view of the snowy city in the morning light.

As I make my way toward the floor-to-ceiling windows, I take in my surroundings. The colors are like his bedroom, muted blues and blacks with white accents. On the walls, there are some pictures. When I get closer, I see they're various events in his life. First, a picture of him and his twin brother Leo when they were a bit younger. Both are in hockey gear and smiling ear-to-ear. It's kind of scary how identical they are. Exact carbon copies, almost. Though I know right away which one Lucas is because I spent all last night looking into his eyes. He has a certain depth to them that his brother lacks, like he's an old soul—I don't know how to explain it.

The next few are pictures of his family on various trips and holidays. When I get to the end of the wall, I notice an award for Best Talent Representation of the Year. But it's not the award itself that makes me stop, it's the name on it: Leo McKnight. I scrunch my nose and try to understand why he'd have his brother's award on the wall.

Does Leo live here too sometimes? Jace did say he works with Leo. But that's still a little odd to have your brother's award on the wall. Lucas must have plenty of his own. Now that I think of it, it's strange he doesn't have any awards related to his hockey accomplishments on display.

Hands wrap around my stomach, and I jump in surprise.

"Merry Christmas, Riley." Lucas's voice tickles my ear. "You stole my slippers."

My hand flies to my chest, my heart racing. "You scared the shit out of me."

He kisses my neck and then my cheek, turning me around in his arms so we're face-to-face. His breath smells like fresh mint, and his dark hair is perfectly mussed. It's criminal how good he looks for having just woke up. And did I mention he's back in a Henley and sweatpants? But this time, they're a beautiful navy color that make his ice blue eyes pop. "Sorry." He grins, though I'm positive he's not. "I woke up and had to come find my slipper-stealer."

I look down at the slippers, laughing at how huge they look on my size nine feet. I shrug. "Your floors are cold."

He chuckles, tugging me away from his wall of weird like he's on a mission and back toward the kitchen. I think about asking him about the award, but decide against it. My plans for surprising the guys with breakfast is now out of the window, and I still need my cup of coffee.

"Making pancakes?" he asks.

"No, I was making pizza."

He lifts one of those pretty black eyebrows at me. "You're hilarious in the mornings."

"Wrong," I chuff. "I'm hilarious all the time."

He shakes his head with mirth and walks to the coffee machine, grabbing the now full cup and handing it to me. I take the offered brew and have the sudden urge to kiss him, so I do. It's short and sweet, not nearly long enough but it also sets my body on fire.

"Merry Christmas," I whisper, pulling back.

"Merry Christmas," he answers.

"You already said that."

He blows out a breath, then kisses my nose. "Like I said, hilarious." Then he steps back to make his own cup.

As he works, I lean back against the kitchen counter to study him. He's meticulous in the way he does his coffee, just like he was with shaving my legs. He sets it to a darker brew and as it pours, he gets out a bottle of cream and a spoon. Once the cup is full, he adds in three little spoonfuls, then stirs it in exactly three times.

"Do you do everything in threes?" I tease him.

He turns to me, coffee now in hand. "Maybe it's my lucky number."

"So you're telling me I'm lucky?"

"Are you?" he challenges.

I sip my coffee before setting the cup on the counter. "Lucky? No. But did I get lucky last night? Yes." His warm amusement fills the chilly room, and my toes curl in his slippers.

"Speaking of lucky," I say, "our flight is back on for two o'clock today. You may want to book your seat before it fills up."

I think disappointment flashes across his face before he wipes it away and smiles. "That's great. I'm sure your family will be happy."

"Won't yours be?"

He nods. "Of course. They love Christmas."

"You never really told me why you don't, by the way."

He places our mugs on the counter so he can crowd me. His face closes in on me so our lips are a whisper away, then he places his hands on my bare ass cheeks. He groans, his cock growing against the swell of my belly. "The holiday season is a busy time of year for me. It's not exactly fun."

"A lot of games?" I ask. I don't miss the way his body tenses, and it makes me think of that award with Leo's name on it again.

"Just a lot of stuff going on."

When I open my mouth to say something, the sound of footsteps stops me. Lucas looks up, and I notice the way his eyes smile.

"Good morning," Jace rumbles in a sleep-laden voice.

I turn in Lucas's arms to find him grinning groggily at us. "Merry Christmas," I chirp.

Jace's eyes look us both up and down, and he licks his lips. "Am I interrupting something?"

Lucas's grip on my waist tightens, and I don't miss the way he rubs his cock into my heating core. "I was just about to ask Shortcake if we could have a little pre-breakfast snack," he replies.

My skin gets warmer, and if I was wearing any panties, I know they'd be wet. With Jace now awake, it's like she has a mind of her own. Both my ass and pussy clench around nothing, greedy for their cocks again.

Jace approaches, his tattooed torso on display as he casually rubs his cock through his sweats. "Are you up for some morning fun, beautiful? You left us all alone in bed, so I wasn't sure you were feeling well enough."

Lucas brushes his thumb over the apple of my cheek. "If you're too sore, we don't have to do anything. Last night was a lot." I know he's actually concerned for me, but I don't miss the shit-eating grin he's wearing while he asks it.

Jace strokes his hand down my arm, fingering the hem of my shirt. Well, his shirt. His eyes look hungry, almost possessive when they return to mine.

One last time can't hurt, right? Just one more fantasy with these two men before I'm on a plane home tonight. Jace's hand cups my pussy, and I can't help the hiss that escapes my mouth.

"I think that's a no for pound-town." Lucas chuckles. "You're okay right?"

My heart swells at his concern. "Perfect. But I have an idea."

They both look at me with a curious expression, and I decide it's now or never. I've committed to my idea. Just this one last dirty fantasy that I thought I'd never do or even ask for.

"Shortcake?" Lucas asks.

But instead of answering, I pull the shirt over my head and throw it to the floor. Then I drop to my knees in front of them and say two words:

"Use me."

CHAPTER SEVENTEEN

Leo

I GO FROM PARANOID Riley has figured out my secret to turned on so fast my head is spinning.

"You realize what those two words do to two men like us?" Jace asks, stepping to my side so we're both looking down at her.

"Yes." She nods, her voice already laden with sex.

Last night was incredible. The best sex of my life. I'd even go as far to say it was life changing. Now here we are again, this woman proving further why she was made for us.

Jace takes her jaw, stroking it before he gently slaps her cheek. Riley inhales a surprised gasp before it turns to a keen of pleasure. I bet her pussy is already dripping. And while she might be too sore for sex, Jace and I can still eat her out. I bet she still tastes of me from last night, too. The thought has my cock as hard as rock, pre-cum staining my clean sweats.

"Open your mouth," I command.

She does as she's told, her pretty hole opening wide. It looks warm and inviting. And when she holds her tongue out flat, I spit onto it. To her credit, she doesn't even flinch. Instead, her chest heaves and her pupils dilate with need.

"You want first, J?" I ask, my tone cool, even though inside I'm a raging mess. I want to snap and fuck her hard and fast while Jace takes my ass. But that's for another time.

"Warm our little slut's mouth up," Jace says. "I want to get something."

I smirk, knowing exactly what he's after. While Jace walks off to one of the closets nearby, I bend down to kiss Riley. It's hard and fast, a kiss that has her panting and wanting more. But I pull back and stand up before it can go too far.

"If you want us to stop at any time, say red. Understand?"

"Yes, Sir."

"Good girl. Now take out my cock and suck me good."

Riley wastes no time, pushing the band of my sweatpants down and freeing me. When her lips encircle my crown, my hands fly to her hair and grip the coppery-blonde strands.

"Fuck, baby. Your mouth feels so good on my cock," I keen.

She hums as she works me deeper in. She's even more confident than she was by the end of last night, sucking me like it's the only job she's ever had.

Jace comes back, he's carrying the red rope I'd first imagined her tied up in. Her eyes flick to his as she brings her hands up to grip the swell of my thighs, but I stop her.

"Did I say you could touch me? I said suck me, Shortcake."

Her nostrils flare a little, but she gets back to work, putting her hands down. When she sees the rope, I know she wants to ask what he's going to do, so I hold her face and gently start to fuck it.

"I think our little slut needs her hands tied, don't you, baby?" Jace asks me. "A little reminder that she's to do as she's told."

I make a show like I'm thinking about it. "She did want us to use her, after all." I pull my cock from her mouth and Jace moves her forward so he has room to work behind her.

He's always been a skilled Rigger. He told me once that he learned it in college from a secret Shibari club. I had laughed at the time, but leave it to Jace to find a club like that in college instead of something normal like kickball or some shit.

Riley waits patiently while Jace works, looping the red rope in a simple double-column tie so her hands are now secured behind her back. After he checks his work to make sure it's not too tight, he steps back to admire her submission.

"Such a pretty thing in ropes, don't you think?" Jace asks.

I walk around her to inspect it, standing in front of Riley so she can see my face while I say, "She'll look even better with a cock or two in her mouth."

Jace laughs loudly before pulling down his own sweats. His swollen cock slaps against his lower belly as he approaches Riley's waiting mouth. "Did we say you could close that pretty hole?" he chuffs.

She shakes her head then opens her mouth for him. Instead of sticking his cock inside, he puts two of his fingers down her throat and presses on her tongue gently.

"When you asked us to use you, is this what you really wanted?" he questions her.

She nods in a short burst. That's all the encouragement Jace needs to move his fingers further down her throat until she gags.

"You want us to fuck your mouth then paint you with our come, beautiful?" he croons.

I can see her arousal glimmering between her thighs as she whines a needy yes.

"Good girl," he praises. Then he replaces his fingers with that monstrous cock of his.

I stroke myself as I enjoy the sight of him using her. Her eyes have begun to water and her hair is a mess from mine and now Jace's hands in it.

"Isn't her mouth amazing, J?" I ask, coming to stroke one of my hands down his back.

"Fucking heaven."

"You look like you're meant to suck his cock, Shortcake. Your big tits are gonna look so good painted with our come."

She tries to rub her thighs together for some relief of her own but fails. It's kind of cute. But she wanted us to use her, so her pleasure will have to come later. I focus my attention back on Jace, running my hands over his arms and tracking the lines of a turtle shell tattoo on his back. He shivers, cursing as he continues to fuck Riley's mouth. When my hands reach the crack of his ass, I run a finger over his tight hole, and he bucks.

Riley gags and he tosses his head back in pleasure.

"Yeah, baby, just like that," Jace moans. I don't know if he's talking to me or Riley, but maybe it's both of us. I continue to tease him, even slipping the tip of my thumb inside a bit.

Jace glares at me. "Are you trying to make me blow my load before you?"

"Is it working?" I tease.

He pulls out of Riley's mouth and slaps my ass. "Tag, you're it."

I give him my one-dimpled smile and replace his cock with mine. Riley's cheeks are red from the work Jace made her do, but she's so sexy like this. Open and ready to please us. I don't know what we're going to do after she leaves, but I'm still holding out hope this morning is not the end for us.

Jace moves behind me and slides his cock up and down my ass, effectively turning my brain into mush.

"Taste of your own medicine," he says against my ear.

I bite my cheek to stop from laughing while I put my hands on the base of Riley's skull and make sure I have eye contact with her before I turn my strokes rougher.

"You're amazing, Riley," I tell her honestly. "Never let anyone tell you anything otherwise." The words might be too serious for what we're doing right now, but they feel right to say nonetheless. Adoration flashes in her irises, and I stroke my thumbs down her jaw.

"I wish I could get a painting of this," Jace hums against my ear. "My pretty boy face-fucking our Shortcake. I'd call it *Santa Came to Town*. So sweet yet so fucking dirty." He grinds his cock into my ass again while biting my neck.

My orgasm edges closer and I step aside so there's room for Jace.

"Suck them both," I order.

Riley smiles around my cock then I pull out so Jace can push back in. After a few thrusts I move in and we continue our pace, taking turns feeling her tight wet hole around us. We each have a hand on her head now while she goes to town. It's a sight to watch, and Jace is right: This should be a painting. Maybe I will have one commissioned like I imagined last night.

"I'm getting close." Jace grunts, his hips slowing as his orgasm builds.

"Me too," I say.

Jace reaches down and fondles my balls. "Suck on them," he tells Riley. She does as she's told without hesitation, her warm mouth wrapping around and sucking me as Jace feeds them to her.

"Goddamn it," I curse, my cock twitching.

The sound of Riley slurping and her little whines as she tries to balance on her knees with her hands tied has my orgasm rushing at me.

"I'm going to come," I shout. I can hear Jace jacking his cock faster and faster as Riley sucks on my balls then moves down my shaft. A moment later she puts her mouth on Jace and he fucks her hard for a few seconds, making her choke on his cock until he pulls out with a cry.

"I'm coming, too. Fucking come with me, Leo!" he shouts.

I grab my cock just as thick ropes of come jet from my cock onto Riley's face and chest. The moment the white liquid hits her pale skin, Jace is coming in endless spurts all down her breasts. We both squeeze our cocks for as long as possible while we watch Riley lick our essence from her lips and savor the taste. It's goddamn kinky and so fucking hot I would come again if I could. Instead I close my eyes and bask in the high of my orgasm and sex hormones in the air.

The sound of Jace and Riley's heavy breathing is eventually what brings me back down to earth. When I open my eyes, Jace is moving to release Riley from her binds and I go to grab a wet towel to wipe her off before I take her into the shower to eat her out in thanks and appreciation. But when I go to wipe her face off, she takes the towel from my hand.

"I can do it," she says stiffly.

"I want to—"

"I said, I can do it," she snaps. When Jace offers his hand to help her up, I notice that he's avoiding my gaze now, too. Did something happen that I'm not aware of?

Worried, I ask, "Did I hurt you, Riley?"

Jace's eyes connect with mine and they look fucking sad and apologetic. My brain goes through what just happened, and then it hits me. Jace called me Leo. Fuck. Fucking, fuck. Fuck!

"Riley," my tone comes out already pleading, "I was going to tell you."

After cleaning herself off, she snatches Jace's shirt off the floor and puts it over her head. When she eventually faces me, her eyes aren't angry, they're disappointed. Which is worse.

"So it's true, then?" she asks.

My gut feels like rocks are being tumbled inside it. I rub the back of my neck nervously. "You thought I was Lucas. It happens to me all the time and I just went with it."

She runs a hand through her messy hair. "Why didn't you just tell me the truth?"

I quickly find my sweatpants and put them back on while Jace does the same. This isn't exactly the kind of conversation you want to have naked. "Look, I know I should have said something. But you were so excited about who you thought I was. I didn't think that it mattered at the time."

"And even after you decided to bring me home, you didn't think I should know then?"

"I thought we'd have last night, then it would be done." The words are sour on my tongue but it's true. At the time I didn't think this would lead to feelings. To wanting more. I did eventually, but we were in too deep by then. Fuck. There's so much more I want to say, but as I play it through my head, it all sounds crazy. Who falls for someone in less than twenty-four hours?

She huffs. "I see." When her gaze turns to Jace, she looks even more disappointed. "And you went along with it?"

Jace grimaces, so I step in. "Jace wanted to tell you, but I asked him not to."

Her chin drops to her chest and she shakes her head solemnly. "I trusted you both."

"We're still the same men, Riley," I insist. "Nothing has changed."

She throws up her hands. "Everything has changed! I thought you were your brother. And you," she points at Jace, "you were in on the whole thing. I feel so stupid."

"You're not stupid, Riley." Jace tries to comfort her, but his voice sounds panicked. Probably from the prospect of losing her. "It's us. We're the stupid ones. I'm so, so, sorry."

"You both fucking *lied*," she spits.

I can't help what happens next. All of my insecurities bubble to the surface, and I snap. "Because you thought I was Lucas is exactly why I didn't tell you! You wanted my brother at the airport. You wanted a night with the hottest fucking bachelor on planet earth. I gave you that."

"Leo," Jace warns, his tone angry. "You're being a dick, and I suggest you stop talking."

I scowl at him, pissed that he's right. And pissed at myself for creating this whole situation. But most importantly, hurting Riley. I shouldn't have said what I said, but I can't take it back.

Riley's eyes turn glassy. "I didn't care about spending a night with Lucas McKnight!" she cries. "I liked you. I liked you because you were kind and funny and YOU. Not because I thought you were Lucas."

I mull over her words. Even though I know I should believe her, I can't help wonder if she's being truthful. When she met me last night, if I told her I wasn't him, would she have stayed? And if she did, would it have been for me and not in hopes of meeting Lucas? The amount of times that any gender has tried to get to my brother through me is more than I can count. I've been burned too often by people I thought I trusted. Can I really trust Riley now? My heart is screaming yes, but my logical brain isn't convinced.

"I don't know what to say," I finally breathe out.

"Seriously?" She blinks at me. "That's all?"

When I open my mouth, nothing comes out. It's not because I don't have anything to say, it's because I'm heeding Jace's warning. If I say something hurtful, I'll make it all worse. And Riley doesn't deserve my bullshit issues, nor can I articulate anything other than said issues right now.

She blows out a shaky breath. "You really fucking used me, didn't you, *Leo*?"

"Riley—"

"No!" she cries. "You fucking used me, just like Chad. You both took advantage of me and my vulnerabilities. I thought... fuck. I don't know what I thought, but what you two did isn't right!"

Jace tries to grab her hand, but she yanks it away from him.

"Don't touch me!" she screams.

The hair on the back of my neck stands up from the sound, and I want nothing more than to hold her. But I can't.

Jace steps back and surrenders. "I'm so sorry, Riley. Please, just sit down with us and we can talk about it. I know what we did isn't good, but after what happened between the three of us, I think we should talk. We all deserve that."

She stares at him, then back to me. "No, I'm not going to do that. I'm going to go clean up and you two are going to leave me the hell alone. Then I'm going to leave and pretend like this night never happened."

"Please, Riley," Jace tries again, the crack in his voice threatening to break me.

She shakes her head. "You two deserve each other."

Then she's storming off down the hallway toward the guest room, the bang of the door slamming in her wake.

After a heavy pause, one that threatens to strangle me, Jace makes eye contact with me. I rarely ever see him angry, but now is not one of those times. He looks pissed. Disappointed. Ready to blow.

"She's right, you know," he says. "We deserve each other."

"And what does that mean?"

"We both realized what was happening last night between the three of us, and we should've come clean. Now it's over with no way to fix it. Now it's only us again, Leo. Are we going to go back to the same 'together, not together' shit again?"

I clench my fists at my sides. Suddenly, everything is too much again. "I can't do this right now, Jace."

He chuckles sadly. "Will you ever be able to?"

I blink at him, my throat closing from the emotion I see on his face. "I don't know."

Then I'm the one walking away—and I fucking hate myself for it.

CHAPTER EIGHTEEN

Jace

I SIP EGGNOG SPIKED with Okolehao that one of my cousins sent me by the fire, the thick sugary drink feeling like tar on my tongue. Usually I savor this drink, as it's part of the Christmas Day traditions I've created for myself since moving to the mainland, but not tonight. Instead, I have the urge to throw it into the crackling flames.

After what went down this morning, and Riley left without a goodbye, Leo decided to leave for Seattle tomorrow and went for "a walk to think" hours ago and hasn't returned. If he hadn't texted that he was fine, I would've thought he had frozen to death. I, on the other hand, cancelled my plans with some of our friends in the city and wallowed. I didn't even eat the Laulau I special ordered—I didn't really eat anything, for that matter.

My stomach aches as I look up at the ceiling, imagining Riley in a plane flying overhead. I still can't believe flights went out today, but I guess Christmas still had a little magic left to give our girl—no, Riley.

I breathe out a dramatic sigh, the moment everything went wrong replaying in my mind. It was idiotic in the first place to not tell her the truth. She thought she was having sex with me and Lucas, not Leo. She put her trust in us, we even asked for her trust, yet we were lying the whole time. I let my hormones and overwhelming attraction to her cloud my judgement. We even went bare, for fuck's sake. If I was her, I would be mad too. She had every right to walk out on us the way she did. And if I'm being realistic, she doesn't owe us anything. We just met.

So despite the Riley-shaped hole that now resides in my heart, I have to come back to reality. Riley is an experience I'll never forget—that we'll never forget. I need to stop pretending like we live in some fairytale where you meet someone and everything just works out. That's not how life works. Leo and I have been together for years, and yet we can't even call ourselves partners or boyfriends. The urge to throw my glass in the fire grows stronger, but I resist.

As I'm about to call it a night and try to get some sleep, the door opens and Leo walks in. He's wrapped in his designer bomber jacket and a thick scarf, his cheeks pink from the cold and dark hair tousled from the wind. Despite how pissed I am at him, I can't deny that all I want to do is apologize for what was said earlier and hold him. I'd like to spend the last part of Christmas pretending like this morning ended on a good note instead of a horrible dumpster fire.

I look back at the dancing flames and close my eyes, willing myself to stay in my seat. If he wants to talk, he'll come to me. That's how Leo has always worked. If it wasn't clear by his reaction to our argument this morning, he's not good at expressing his feelings or dealing with whatever is going on in his head. That's why I never push.

But after what went down last night, and what Riley said to us, I couldn't not say something. Leo needed to hear my feelings vocalized by me. Was I sad that he walked away? Yes. But I also expected it. At least he's here now and didn't fly to an island somewhere to avoid everything.

As I wait to see what he chooses, I listen to him take off his coat and boots before heading to the kitchen. His footsteps sound heavier than usual, almost like he's dragging his feet across the wood floors. When the coffee machine whirs to life, I know he's going to talk. He wouldn't drink caffeine after seven unless he needs to be awake and alert.

After a few more drawn out minutes that feel like torture, he surprises me by taking a seat on the cushion next to me. I can't help the comfort I feel when our thighs touch.

We don't immediately say anything; instead, we watch the flames of the fire and sip our drinks. Eventually, the sound of his cup meeting the coffee table has me turning my gaze. His blue eyes are dull with sadness and slightly bloodshot.

My chest tightens. "Were you walking this whole time? You've been out all day," I say with worry.

He shakes his head. "I went to the movie theater and paid for whatever was playing. I have no idea what I watched. Then I walked through Central Park until it was dark and then up and down some streets until I couldn't feel my face."

I stroke my free hand through my beard and let his words settle over me. "You're really torn up about this, aren't you?" I ask after a minute.

He blinks at me like that should be obvious, even though I honestly wasn't sure, given he didn't fight for Riley—or me—earlier. A fact that I can't forget but also understand. "And you aren't?" he asks.

A tense breath leaves my lips, and I set my near-empty glass down. "You know I am. But I spent the entire day alone thinking about the last twenty-four hours. Last night was...honestly, there are no words. But at the same time, I can't help but wonder if maybe we took it too far."

He looks at me as if I just told him the sky is blue. "Of course we did. But it was my fault, Jace. Not yours."

I shake my head. "No, not that."

"Then what?" he asks curiously.

"We brought Riley into a world that was entirely new to her. On Christmas Eve no less, and after she had a terrible day. I think we all got caught up in the moment and the magic of it all. It was spontaneous and new and fun. She's also funny and beautiful. It was a perfect night. But maybe that's all it was. All it was meant to be. I think we need to let her go and work on our own shit, Leo. She doesn't deserve to be involved in our bullshit. She's too good for that."

Leo shakes his head like he's disagreeing with me. Then he leans forward and places his hand over my heart. "Is that how you feel here, Jace?"

I look at him in astonishment. He's the last person who would ever tell someone to follow their heart. Dick? Yes. Heart? Absolutely not. Especially after how our conversation ended this morning.

"Did something happen to you while you were walking that I should know about? Maybe you were visited by the Ghosts of Christmas?"

The corners of his lips turn up. "No visits to see Tiny Tim, I'm afraid. But I did realize something."

I place my hand over the one he has on my chest. "And what's that?"

"That I've been a total asshole. A total fucking oblivious *and* selfish asshole."

I think I stop breathing. "Can you repeat that? I'm not sure I heard you."

He clucks his tongue. "Dick, don't make me say it twice."

I squeeze his hand, not quite believing he's about to have the conversation I think he's about to have with me.

"And what have you been oblivious and selfish about?" I ask cautiously.

He sighs tiredly. "You're really going to make me go deep, aren't you?"

I wink. "You know I like deep."

He barks out a laugh. "Only you would crack a joke right now."

"And maybe one other person with a banging body and strawberry-blonde hair?" I dare to say.

A wistful expression colors his features. "You're not wrong there."

I place our hands on his thigh, running my thumb across his knuckles. "Tell me, Leo. I want to hear whatever you have to say."

He stares at our joined hands, studying the veins and skin until he exhales a shaky breath. "I've been oblivious about what you really mean to me, Jace. Yesterday morning, I woke up thinking everything we had was exactly how it was meant to be. For the last few years we work, travel, sometimes we don't see each other for weeks but when I come home you're always here, and when I leave you're often still here," he teases.

I shrug. "What? You have a better place. More amenities."

He pinches my thigh with his free hand and I swat him away. "I'm trying to be serious here!"

"I know, I am being serious. Now go on."

He rolls his eyes again, but I know it's helping that I've lightened the mood. This is big for him, and I want him to feel comfortable. "I've based our unique relationship status on the detail that we're both commitment-phobes, when really I think I've avoided calling you my boyfriend because I didn't think I could do it."

My body tenses. "What do you mean?"

He skims my knuckle for a beat before speaking. "My entire life, I've lived in Lucas's shadow. He's always been funnier, more charming, and got better grades. On top of that, I wasn't straight like the world expected me to be. It was like the universe decided to pick him to have an easier life. The one thing I had that I was better at was hockey. So when I got injured sophomore year, and then Lucas got drafted, I finally accepted that the life I dreamed of since I played my first game of pee-wee just wasn't in the cards for me."

He turns our hands over and traces the lifeline on my palm. "That night I met you, it was the lowest I've felt. I knew my injury would never let me play at the level I needed to go pro, and I thought my life was over. Then you sat down next to me at that shitty bar that always took fake IDs. You knew my stats and you knew about my injury, and I thought you were a fucking creep. But then you said you were planning to be a sports agent and, well, you know how the rest of the story goes."

"I might have been stalking you a little bit," I blurt out.

Leo stares at me. "Really?"

I tell him what I've already known for so long. "I mean, can you blame me? If I'm being honest, I had a crush on you. I couldn't really admit it to myself yet, but of course there was a bigger reason why I knew your career like the back of my hand."

He nods, his lips turning up slightly like he already knew that.

"But what does this have to do with our relationship?" I ask.

He swallows, his Adam's apple bobbing in nervousness. "When we talked about your desire to be an agent, and you mentioned how it could be an option for me, you gave me a pathway that night that allowed me to continue my love of hockey and the industry. Not only that, but you became my best friend and then more. Way more than that. I know it sounds stupid, but I loved hockey. In a way, it was the love of my life. It was my heart and my blood. It was what I was good at and I was never in Lucas's shadow when I was on the ice. Then I lost it."

My heart pounds in my chest at the connections I'm making as he speaks.

He continues, "I think over the years, you became my hockey. I know it sounds stupid because you can't compare a human, especially you, to a game. And I know I tell you I love you, but admitting I love you *that* fucking much, with everything I have, it terrifies me."

My heart feels like it's in a chokehold. What he's saying makes sense. After over ten years of knowing him, loving him, he's never once given me any inclination that this is why he didn't want to fully go all-in with me. He's silent now, back to staring at our hands like maybe if he stares long enough, they'll tell him something.

I reach over and take his face between my palms. His eyes are filled with fear, and I don't think I've ever seen him this close to crying before.

"You don't have to be terrified, baby. I'm not a hockey career or someone who overshadows you. I'm a man who's in love with you. One who has always loved you. You're not going to lose me, Leo."

"Riley is wrong, Jace. I don't deserve you."

I shake my head and put my hands back in his. "That's bullshit, and you know it. We both agreed to stay casual. We've both had our reasons to not shout to the world that we're together and in an open relationship."

"But the only reason you haven't is because I pushed it on you," he argues.

"No. You know my life, Leo. You know that most of my family doesn't speak with me because of who I am. And you know the industry we're in isn't exactly all rainbows and pride parades unless it's Pride Month. I've been scared too. It's not just you."

Everything I'm saying is the truth. I've played a part in our relationship being the way it is. I don't talk about my immediate family much because I have people in my life who care about me more than they ever did. And I'm not scared of being bisexual or people knowing that I am anymore. But the life I lead, the clients Leo and I have, and the companies we work with, it's easier to play the part of a straight and narrow man's man most of the time. But I think it's time to end that crap.

"I think we've both been idiots," I continue. "And instead of trying to lay blame on why we've ended up here instead of happily ever fucking after, we need to decide what it is we want."

Leo smiles slyly. "I know what I want."

I bring my face closer to his so our lips are a breath away. "And what is it that you want?"

"To be with you. No more 'together, not together' shit. No more pretending that you and I are just 'close buddies' at the office. I want it all with you, Jace."

A thrill runs through my entire being. Those are words I've always wanted to hear but shoved the possibility of down, time and time again. He runs his fingers through my beard, then traces my lips.

"But do you want to hear why I've been selfish?" He doesn't give me time to answer. "When I met Riley last night and she thought I was Lucas, it was just a game at first. I took what I wanted and made you play along with my game. I didn't allow myself to think too much of her feelings, or yours. I only thought of myself and how good it felt to pretend I was the man of her fantasy. Then by the time I wish I hadn't, it was too late. Fuck, J. It was stupid. But at the same time, I can't regret it."

I lift a curious eyebrow at him. "And why's that?"

"Because I can't regret anything with Riley. Or anything that happened between the three of us. It was—"

"Fucking perfect," I finish for him.

He nods. "Ever since she walked out this morning, it's like there's something missing."

At Leo's words, I rub the space in my chest that feels empty, and he watches with a pained face.

"How is that possible when we just met her, Jace?" he asks, his voice thick with emotion.

I brush some hair away from his eyes. "Love at first sight is a real thing, baby. I know because it's happened to me once already."

Leo's eyes soften. "You've always been ahead of the game."

"Talent," I tease.

He shakes his head. "This makes things complicated, you know?"

"And when has life not been complicated?"

"True, but is this what you want?" he implores.

I think of Riley's trusting pine green eyes and the way her soft body felt between us last night. How we moved in a symbiotic way that felt like we'd known each other for years. Of how she dropped to her knees for us this morning like it was natural and normal. I've been trying to convince myself all day that it was just one night and to get over it, but when I really let myself feel what it would be like to never see her again, or hear her musical voice, the hole in my chest grows exponentially. Is it crazy to want and need someone that much after less than a day? Yes. But I've never claimed to be sane.

"Riley is ours," I say with conviction. *Our girl*.

Leo's eyes light up, the mischievous glint that's usually in them returning. "I think so, too," he confirms.

I grip his hands. "She may not want us, Leo. You need to prepare yourself for that. We don't exactly come without baggage or a lifestyle change."

A dreamy look reflects in his blue eyes. "I think she'll understand. I know she will," he says.

Maybe something really did happen to him on that walk and he doesn't remember. He's usually not hopeful and optimistic. Especially when it comes to trusting people.

"You're willing to go all in, Leo? Because if we ask her to come into our lives, all the random sex and group activities, it stops unless we all agree it's something we want together."

"I don't want anyone else but you and her, Jace. If I didn't know it this morning, I sure as hell knew it last night." He takes my jaw between his fingers. "I told you once and I'll tell you again and again until you believe me. I want it all with you, Jace."

I blink at him. "I feel like I'm living in an alternate reality."

This time he gives me the one-dimpled smile I fell in love with all those years ago.

"Maybe it's just the magic of Christmas," he says.

"Now I know I'm dreaming, Mr. Scrooge."

He leans forward so our lips are barely a whisper away. "You're not dreaming."

When his mouth finally touches mine, our kiss is slow and tentative at first. It reminds me of the first time I ever kissed a man. It's sweet and innocent, wholly unlike my usual kisses with Leo. He cups my cheek and slides his fingers through my beard, my body shivering at his touch.

Slowly, he coaxes my mouth open and his tongue slides in, tasting and exploring tenderly. I can't help but feel like this kiss means more than any kiss we've ever had. It's full of apologies and promises, but even better—love. When we pull back, everything is different, and yet nothing has changed.

"What do you say, J?" Leo breathes against my lips. "You, me, two seats to Seattle, and if we're lucky, we'll be back before New Year's with a strawberry-blonde beauty in between us."

"Did you already buy the tickets?" I ask.

He scoffs. "You think I'm an amateur?"

I pull him by the shirt and plant a solid kiss on his lips. "I'm all in, pretty boy. When do we leave?"

CHAPTER NINETEEN

Riley

I STARE UP AT the ceiling of my childhood bedroom. Well, it's not really my bedroom anymore. After I moved to New York for good, Mom turned it into her sewing room but kept my bed in it along with some of my decorations—including the burgundy walls I begged for when I was fifteen.

"Your mood matches your room."

Chuckling, I lift my head off the pillows to find Stevie standing in the doorway. She's got on the ugly Christmas sweater I gave her that says "Merry Christmas Ya Filthy Animal," and has two cups of what I'm assuming is hot cocoa in her hands.

I sit up and move over on the queen-sized bed so she can join me, taking the green mug from her hand. I've done my best over the last day and a half to pretend like everything was normal and I didn't just have the wildest night of my life followed by one of the craziest mornings. But I knew Stevie saw through it the moment I walked through the door last night. We're only two years apart and talk almost every day. The woman can read me like a book.

We sit in silence for a few minutes, sipping the sweet drink. Eventually she clears her throat, flipping her long brown hair over one of her shoulders.

"Are you going to tell me why you've been acting like someone kicked your puppy since you got home?"

"I don't have a puppy."

She tuts. "Spill, sister. What happened between Christmas Eve and now? Did you not get that work account or something?

I shake my head. "No, we got the account."

"Did Chad do something again? I swear to God I'll fly to New York right now and kick his ass."

"I mean, I'd pay money to see that. And yes, Chad always does something—but it's not him."

Stevie scrutinizes me with her green eyes before a smile plays at her lips. My cheeks heat up; it's like she can tell just by looking at me that I had two dudes banging me on one of the holiest nights of the year.

"Does this have anything to do with the hickey I saw you covering up this morning?"

My eyes bug out of my head, and I start to sweat. Stevie and I share a bathroom when we stay at home, and I was stupid enough not to lock the door this morning. Thankfully, I had my clothes on when she barged in to pee, but I was in the process of covering up a bite mark that one of the guys had given me near the collar of my sweater. I thought I got lucky and she didn't see it.

"Aha!" she exclaims so loud I jump. "You did have sex. Please tell me it wasn't with Chad!"

"No! Oh God, no."

She squeals. "Then with who, you little slut!?"

"Shhh!" I cry. My cheeks turn redder from the memory of the last two people who called me that. "Keep your voice down."

"Mom and Dad fell asleep in front of the TV like they always do after dinner. They're not going to hear us. So who was it? Did you join the Mile High Club or something?"

As I stare at Stevie, her eyes glimmering with excitement, I think about how thrilled I was to tell her about meeting Lucas. How I had the whole scene in my head where I told her I got to bang her fantasy man and all-time hockey crush. It was going to be the one thing she'd always be jealous of (in a fun, sister kind of way). Now, contrary to what Leo might think, I'm not upset that he wasn't Lucas. That's not it at all. I'm upset because he lied to me. Because Jace lied to me. My eyes start to fill with tears before I can stop them.

Alarmed, Stevie takes my mug and sets our drinks on the bedside table before pulling me into a hug. When her warm soft body envelops mine, I can't hold it in any longer. The tears start flowing and my body shakes with silent sobs.

"Ri, what the hell happened? You never cry like this."

She's right. I've never been a huge ugly crier, always more of a "stuff your emotions down" type of gal. Even after everything Chad did, all of his lies and cheating and bullshit behavior, the most I ever did was let my eyes turn glassy before I blinked it all away. But now I can't stop my tear ducts from acting up over two men I've known for less than a day.

"It's stupid," I mutter into her shoulder.

"It's not stupid if you're this upset. Tell me who hurt you so I can kill them."

I laugh, pulling away so I can wipe the tears from my cheeks. Then I try and figure out how to tell her everything that happened. I know she won't judge me, but the whole thing got complicated the moment I let my emotions get involved.

She squeezes my shoulder so I'll look at her. When we make eye contact, all I can see is genuine concern in her green eyes. The concern of a sister who just wants her sibling to be okay—so I let it spill out.

"I had a threesome with Leo McKnight and his best friend."

The room is silent as Stevie stares at me, her expression blank. For a minute, I think she's gone comatose, but then she lets out a booming cackle. Loud enough that she for sure woke Mom and Dad.

"Oh wow. You had me there!" She slaps her knee. "But seriously, what's going on?"

"I'm serious, Stevie. Like, pinky-swear serious."

She stops laughing, her eyes boring into mine as she tries to spot a lie. "You're not joking?"

I gesture to my splotchy tear-stained face and then pull the neck of my sweater down so she can see the other marks on top of my cleavage. "Does this look like I'm joking?"

"Holy shit, Riley. You're serious."

"Dead serious."

She leans back against the bed frame and stares at my emo burgundy wall in shock. "Out of all the things you could have said to me, that was never on my radar."

"I can honestly say the same," I chuff.

"You had a threesome with my fantasy man's identical twin and his friend. What the flying fuck."

I can't help the giggle that escapes me at her choice of words. "Are you upset?" I ask.

She smirks, her body turning back to mine. "Upset? Fuck no. Jealous, hell yeah. I'm just trying to figure out how that even happened. You said you went home on Christmas Eve."

"I went to a home, but that home was not mine."

She fully turns toward me now, excited. "Was she hot?"

"She?" I ask.

"His friend. Was she hot?"

My cheeks flush. "His friend is a man. And yes, he's hot."

"Oh my god!" She gasps. "Oh my god! This is insane, Riley. Like really insane."

"I know."

"Tell me everything, and not because I want to know, I actually NEED to know. But more importantly, I need to know why the hell you're so upset after a threesome with Leo McKnight and his hot friend."

I let out a long sigh. "I think we're going to need something stronger than hot cocoa for this story. And also," I stare at the open door, "more privacy."

She grins toothily. "I have an idea."

* ❋ ❋ *

An hour later, we're sitting at some sports bar downtown. You'd be surprised how many places in a big city are closed early the day after Christmas. So this was our only option. The place is fairly busy, but we managed to find a booth in the back where I've just laid out the events of the night to Stevie.

"So you're really telling the truth. You met Leo McKnight at an airport bar and you went back to his penthouse where you, his friend Jace, and him, all got busy until Santa came down the chimney?"

I have to try not to roll my eyes. "Well yes, but we also did some stuff in the morning." My body turns hot at the memory of me on my knees, my hands tied behind my back, and their come dripping all over my body. I still can't believe I asked for that. Yet, I loved every second of it. Until the very last moment.

"You dirty horndog. I had no idea you had it in you!"

I take a sip of my beer. "Me either. I'd like to blame all the drinks I had, but I wanted it."

"Hey, liquid courage isn't always a bad thing. As long as you weren't so intoxicated you couldn't make good choices. But a threesome with two dudes on Christmas Eve sounds like the dirty D-list Christmas movie of my dreams. So, good choice."

I let out a laugh. Stevie has always been more adventurous and outgoing than me. She probably would have been the one instigating a three-way instead of the one being asked to join. Warmth fills me, and I'm glad I was able to come home. Not just to see my family for the holiday, but also to talk this through. If I was in New York, I would have drowned myself in work to forget. I have a few friends I could have talked to, but this isn't something you just share with anyone.

"But your story still doesn't answer the question of why you cried, Riley. I would think someone who just got taken to pound-town by two hotties would be on cloud nine. What happened?"

Stupid tears threaten to fall from my eyes again despite her ludicrous words. "There's one part I left out."

She smirks. "One of them has a third nipple?"

I shove her shoulder. "Wow! So mature."

"Okay, okay. Tell me. I'll behave."

I sigh. "When I first met Leo at the airport, I thought he was Lucas. I told him you were a big fan of his and then we just got to talking. Then you know the rest."

"You told him I was a big fan? OMG, what did he say?"

"Focus, Stevie! We're talking about me."

She gestures for me to continue with a roll of her wrist. "Right, right, go on."

"He never corrected me. I thought he was Lucas the whole time. I called him Lucas the entire night we were together. And Jace didn't say anything either. He even called him Lucas to keep up the ruse."

Stevie taps the table with her red painted fingernails. "And that upset you?"

She says it so calmly I start to question if maybe I'm making too big of a deal out of it. "I mean, yeah. I thought I was sleeping with someone else. They both lied to me about it."

Her fingernails move to tap the side of her pint, her brain processing something. The tapping is starting to annoy me. And after she doesn't say anything for another minute, I ask, "Do you have something you want to say?"

She hums. "I'm just curious why it matters. You hardly know them. I thought you said it was a one-night stand. I've given men a fake name before when I've slept with them—can't be too safe these days. It's not really a big deal."

"But this is different, Stevie! I thought he was Lucas McKnight. I slept with him and let him and Jace do things to me I normally wouldn't have because I trusted them. Who does that? Who pretends to be their famous brother during a one-night stand?" By the time I finish, my chest is heaving and I feel a headache coming on.

Stevie holds up her hands in an attempt to slow me down. "Okay, okay. I understand. I'm just trying to give you a new perspective."

I chug my remaining beer. "I'm going to get another. Do you want one?"

She shakes her head almost sadly as I turn to walk off toward the bar. I order a new beer from the bartender and try to calm down. But when my eyes find one of the several TVs above the bar, my heart jumps in my chest when I see Lucas. There's no game on until tomorrow, but the sports casters are talking about the team and his impressive stats. It's strange seeing him because it really is almost the same as looking at Leo. But like I saw in that old photo on Christmas morning, there's a difference. Lucas has more of a golden retriever energy shining through his blue eyes. Like he still enjoys going to keggers and isn't afraid to admit he likes *The Notebook*. Which we stan.

Stevie's question runs through my mind. *And that upset you?* Of course it upset me. And I also expected my little sister to be upset for me. But as I take a few deep breaths and cool off, I realize that even though she knows that Chad cheated on me, she doesn't know all of the times he lied, and still lies to me. I have trust issues, and I put my trust in two men I didn't even know. Which is on me. I made a choice at that airport to come home with Leo, and if I hadn't started to develop feelings in such a short amount of time, I would have left in the morning and never known the truth.

The bartender hands me my beer, and I head back to the booth feeling slightly better. Stevie is typing on her phone when she spots me.

"Someone I know?" I ask.

She eyes me carefully as she says, "Just Dad."

I slide in next to her and let out a sigh. "I'm sorry I snapped, Stevie. It's been a crazy couple of days. I'm just trying to process it all but haven't really had time. It all happened so fast."

Stevie reaches over and squeezes my hand. "It's okay, Ri. I didn't mean to upset you. I swear."

"I know you didn't. I just..." I stare at another TV that now has Lucas on it, like he's haunting me. Stevie's eyes follow my gaze and she taps her fingernails on the table again in a slow rhythm.

"Are you upset that it wasn't Lucas? Is that what it is?" she asks.

"What? No! That's not it at all."

"Then why are you so upset? I'm not trying to make you angry, I'm just trying to understand why my big sister cried for the first time since Mr. Bubbles died."

I can't help but smile at the mention of our beloved pet goldfish that survived a mere twenty-four hours after we won him at the state fair when I was eight and Stevie was six.

I watch the carbonation fizz up through my beer, afraid of the feelings that are swirling in my stomach right now. I look at Lucas on the TV again and I think of Leo. Of how he treated me with such care last night, how his ice-blue eyes always made sure I felt safe and good in my body. Then I think of Jace and his thoughtfulness, the way he called me beautiful.

Stevie lets out a long "*Ohhhhh*" before patting me on the back.

"What?" I ask, confused.

"You're in love with them."

I scoff, a stupid laugh spilling out of me. "That's insane. I just met them."

"Dude, it's 2023. Weirder things have happened than falling in love at first dicking."

A man walks by the table at the same time she says that. My cheeks flush a bright red when he stops to stare at us like we have three heads. But he's also slightly intrigued, like maybe he could have a chance with us.

Stevie coughs, shooing him away. "Move along sir, nothing to see here!"

The man flushes and scurries off, probably to tell his friends what he just heard.

"Maybe talk a little quieter, Stevie."

She brushes away my words in her nonchalant way. "So back to you being in love with two men. Now I get why you've got your Christmas panties in a twist."

God, my sister. She's one of a kind.

"I'm not in love!" I exclaim.

She sips her beer, smiling over the glass. "You're so in love."

"It's called infatuation, Stevie. It was the best sex of my life. They worshiped me, gave me a bunch of orgasms. That's not love."

"I don't know, sounds like something I could fall in love with."

"Be serious for a second!"

"I am being serious. All I hear is a bunch of excuses for you being in love. I know you. I know that you like to be cautious and guard your heart, especially after what Chad did. But Chad doesn't represent all men. And Leo and Jace sound like good guys."

"I hardly know them."

"You can get to know them. Doesn't mean you can't have some love at first sight action. You deserve that, big sister. Especially after what you've been through."

"What you're saying sounds great in theory. But you're forgetting that it's me and two men. How would I explain that to Mom and Dad?"

"You know Mom and Dad are hip with the times. They went to Seattle Pride. Sometimes I think they're Swingers. I saw Mom with an upside down pineapple thing once and never forgot it."

"Oh my god, Stevie! Please stop talking."

"What? If that's what you're worried about, don't be. You're scared and making excuses to protect yourself. Which is totally normal."

I look at her in disbelief. "Since when have you become a relationship guru?"

"I watch a lot of Love Island after work."

I snort. "You're on a roll tonight."

"You're my sister, and I want you to be happy. If Leo and Jace make you happy, then you should see if it can work."

"I don't know, Stevie. I think it's a long shot. I left on bad terms. We didn't even talk about what we did together because I left. They could've been ready to kick me out after breakfast and never see me again. Also, they already have a relationship and history built together, one that's stronger than they even realize. I don't know if Leo and Jace want me in their life."

"And if we do?"

Stevie smiles wide as my body freezes from the sound of a voice that makes me shiver. I turn to look where her eyes are trained, only to find Leo McKnight standing in the same Seattle sports bar as me on the day after Christmas, with Jace right beside him.

CHAPTER TWENTY

Leo

RILEY IS MORE BEAUTIFUL than I remember. I'm not sure how that's possible, since I thought my memory did a pretty good job at capturing her. But now that I'm seeing her in person again, this woman could easily bring me to my knees right in the middle of this bar.

Her pine eyes bounce between Jace and me.

"Hi, Shortcake," I say, giving her a small smile.

She still doesn't say anything, her mouth pressed in a hard line while her sister sits grinning next to her. They look similar with round features and green eyes. If I didn't know they were sisters, it would be hard to miss that they're related. I swallow the lump in my throat as I watch Riley, questions she wants answered written across her face. I'll answer them all if she'll let me, but in private.

The moment I walked into this dime-a-dozen bar, I felt eyes on me. The patrons all think I'm Lucas; of that, I have no doubt. But I didn't make eye contact with anyone, just searched for Riley's strawberry-blonde hair and made a beeline to her booth with Jace in tow.

When Riley continues to not make a sound or any movement, for that matter, Jace reaches for my hand, giving it a reassuring squeeze. The gesture finally seems to break Riley from her shock, and her eyes lock on our joined hands. I don't miss how her gaze softens, or the slight upturn of her pouty lips. I've held Jace's hand before, but never in a crowded bar in my hometown, the very hometown that Lucas plays hockey in. I'm sure the men staring have already been taking pictures. I make a mental note to text Lucas to let him know his publicist should be aware so they can get ahead of the stories that I'm sure will pop up in the tabloids tomorrow.

A clearing of a throat has me looking at her sister. She nudges Riley in the arm. "Are you going to say something, Ri? Because I'm dying from the sexual tension."

Jace lets out a small laugh, his hazel eyes shining.

"You must be Riley's sister," he says.

She half stands, reaching across the booth so she can shake his hand. "The one and only. I'm Stevie, and you must be Jace." She eyes him up and down, biting her lower lip a bit. "Nice work, Sis."

Riley's pink blush colors her cheeks in full force. I have bite back a laugh. Stevie sure doesn't hide who she is.

She nudges her sister again, and Riley finally speaks. "What are you doing here?"

"Isn't it obvious?" Jace's deep voice rumbles. "We're here to get our girl."

I think Stevie makes an *aww* sound, but I'm too lost in Riley's reaction. Her breathing picks up, and her pupils dilate. She's definitely thinking of our night together and of what we did Christmas morning. I know because I'm thinking about it too.

"How did you find me?" she questions.

Stevie sighs dramatically, flipping her long brown hair that's the same wavy texture as Riley's over her shoulder. "Is that really what you care about right now, Ri? This is like a big romantic gesture out of a movie. But if you must know, they showed up at the house and Dad told them where we were. I just saw the text from him while you were at the bar that said they were coming. You left your phone at home, or Dad would've texted you. Now, stop asking questions, and kiss them, or something."

Riley looks mortified at Stevie's words, and while I very much appreciate that she's on Team Throuple, I step in. "You left your work ID at my place with your last name and email. I may have called in a few favors with some tech friends to find out where your parents live. Your dad probably gave up your location way too easily by the way, but I have to say I'm glad he did. We need to talk to you, Riley."

Jace clears his throat to chime in. "What Leo wants to say is, will you give us a chance to make this better? To talk everything through?"

I grip Jace's hand harder as Riley's gaze penetrates us. I have the desire to shy away from the intensity of it. It's like she's staring into our souls, trying to figure out if we mean what we say. But neither Jace nor I look away; instead, we stare back.

After what seems like forever, but is probably a few seconds, she finally nods in agreement, and I let out a breath of relief.

"Not here." I glance behind me at the people staring. "We have a room at the hotel down the street."

She looks confused again, and I can't help but smile. "It wasn't intentional, but I guess the universe wants us to talk. We booked that room before we knew you were here."

"But my sister—"

"I'm fine, Ri," Stevie says, grinning. "I'll take the car and you can Uber home tomorrow."

Fuck, I already love Stevie.

"Are you sure, Stevie?" Riley asks.

She stands, sliding out of the booth. "Positive. Who am I to get in the way of love?"

Her words have the three of us all blooming in color.

When she's in front of us, she stands at her full height and points a finger at us. She's not tall like Riley, maybe 5'5" at most, but she's intimidating.

"Don't make me regret this. I know how to make rumors go viral." She snaps her fingers, and I flinch. "Like that."

Riley abruptly stands, tugging on her coat as she makes her way out of the booth to end her sister's frightening threats.

"Okay, Stevie. I'll see you at home."

"Have fun." She winks. Then she's darting out of the bar, leaving the three of us and a packed room full of Seattle Stormbreaker fans.

Jace looks wearily over his shoulder. "We should probably head out before this turns into an autograph and picture signing."

Riley cringes. Out of all the places in the world, she had to be at a sports bar in downtown Seattle.

"Good idea." I hold out my hand to Riley, and to my surprise, she doesn't hesitate to take it.

When our palms touch, it feels like one of those rom-com movies where the character gets zapped by a spark. The touch of her smooth hand in mine and Jace's rough one in the other has my body ablaze. It feels so fucking right. I'm broken out of my stupor by some drunk yelling that he didn't know Lucas McKnight was into such kinky shit.

Riley squeezes my hand. "Let's go," she says.

She tugs at me and we start to move through the bar, which has only gotten more crowded since we walked in. Some people have their phones out, and others look like they want to ask for an autograph. When a guy approaches us, Riley grips my hand and holds her free one up in a *stop* gesture.

"I'm sorry, but we won't be doing any pictures tonight. We're on our way to a family event," she tells him, her voice kind but strong. Fuck, that was hot. I wonder if she's ever considered being a celebrity publicist. She'd be great at it. It would also get her away from Chad, which thrills me.

Once we're free of the curious crowd and walking into the frigid winter air, I finally take in a frozen breath. "Thanks for that, Shortcake. It was impressive."

"It was nothing."

"It wasn't nothing to me." I squeeze her hand. "Now let's get to the room before we freeze to death."

* ❄ ❄ *

A similar look of awe like the first time she saw the inside of my penthouse washes over Riley's face as she takes in the honeymoon suite of the hotel. It's massive, with white and gold accents throughout the space. There's also complimentary champagne and chocolate-covered strawberries on the king-sized bed for "the happy couple," as the man told Jace and me when we checked in.

I have to admit it was nice he thought we'd just got married. And the fact that the idea of marrying him didn't scare me shows how much everything has changed since we met Riley. I feel like a totally different person. The only thing that will make everything perfect is Riley's forgiveness.

"You went all out, didn't you?" she asks.

"It was the only room we could find open," I say.

Jace chuffs. "Be real, baby. Even if this wasn't the only room left, you still would've gotten the best room they had."

My body heats. "Okay, that may be true."

Jace grins and takes his coat off, draping it over the back of a chair. "Would anyone like a drink?" he asks.

"Yes, please," Riley and I answer at the same time. It makes the three of us laugh and breaks some of the tension.

"Let's sit," I say, taking my own coat off and grabbing hers. When we're seated on the couch, Riley a respectable distance away from me, I have to stop myself from pulling her to me like I would have the other night.

For a brief time we sit in silence, Riley twiddling her thumbs as we wait for Jace with our drinks. I hate that we went from being able to easily talk to acting like strangers. I just hope we can fix it.

"Here you are," Jace says, handing Riley some of the champagne. "And for you." He gives me the other glass before sitting down on the other side of Riley.

Riley thanks him, then takes small sip, her nose scrunching cutely from the tickle of bubbles. After taking a drink, I place my glass down on the coffee table and face her. I'm nervous, but with Jace here, his warm gaze safe and encouraging, I know that no matter what, it's going to be okay.

After a deep breath, I open my mouth to speak, but Riley beats me to it. "I'm sorry," she blurts out.

Jace and I look at her, confused.

"What are you sorry for, Riley?" I ask. "None of this was your fault."

Riley bites her lower lip. "Maybe so, but I think I may have overreacted a bit." She leans back just enough so she can address Jace. "You were right to ask me to stay and talk everything through instead of leaving."

"Riley," he starts, but she shakes her head.

"At the time, I was just too upset to think straight. And honestly, I think I got a little scared. Christmas Eve was..." She looks off into space for a moment, remembering. "It was intense, wonderful, eye-opening. Finding out you both lied just set me off, made all my trauma from Chad come up." She lets out a sad huff that has my chest aching.

"You didn't overreact, Riley," Jace says, his voice like a soothing balm. "While we wish you would've stayed, we should've told you the truth from the beginning. It was wrong of us."

Riley picks at invisible lint on her black leggings. "It hurt. To know you'd both kept that secret after what we shared together. I felt—*feel*—like an idiot."

Fuck. I'm an asshole. A big one.

"No, no, no, Riley," I try to reassure her, "you're not an idiot. If anyone is, it's definitely me. This is ultimately my doing. I should be the only one that feels like an idiot here."

"Actually, I think Chad is the real idiot," Jace adds.

She smiles at him, a breathy laugh leaving her lips. "He really is."

I scoot closer to her on the couch, my body angled toward her so our knees touch. When she doesn't move away, I do an internal fist pump. So I take it one step further and take her hand. That spark happens again, and my heart thumps in my chest.

"You were always honest with us, and we should've been honest with you," I say. "Regardless of how our evening started at the airport, I should've known from the second we all met that you were never going to be a one-night stand, Riley."

She sucks in a sharp breath, and I squeeze her fingers tighter while Jace places a hand on her back. The gesture is hopefully letting her know that he thinks the same as well. "Jace and I talked after you left. He knocked some sense into me."

I give Jace a quick glance, and he answers with a warm smile—one that makes my heart race. "I've come to realize a couple of things since Christmas Eve. One of which is that I've been an oblivious idiot. Jace and I are together, together now. No more bullshit and pretending otherwise."

Riley's face brightens. "About time."

"Damn straight." Jace winks at her.

I want to roll my eyes at their antics, but I don't. I brush my thumb over Riley's knuckles, and she turns her attention back to me.

I continue, "The other is that I've been selfish. I didn't want to disappoint you. You thought I was Lucas, and while it was meant to be harmless at the time, I realize that me not revealing the truth came from shit I've been dealing with my whole life. It has nothing to do with you, Riley. I was wrong for not admitting that I'm just me. I'm Leo."

A thoughtful quiet settles around us. My words, *I'm Leo*, hanging in the air.

Riley shifts, taking her hand from mine to bring it to my jaw. She strokes the stubble that's formed there, then runs her finger along my ear. My whole body quivers at her touch, and I do my best to keep my cock from perking up. This is a serious moment, but it's also my Shortcake touching me. My body has already learned to crave her sweetness.

"I like Leo," she murmurs. "I like him a lot. I couldn't give two shits about you being a famous hockey player or an actor. I wanted to go home with you because you made me feel good. I felt safe enough to put my well-being in your hands for the night." She glances at Jace, then offers her free hand to him, which he gladly takes. "And yours, Jace." When she looks back at me, there's a seriousness in her eyes that conveys to me the importance of what she's saying. "I don't care who you are or what you do for a living, Leo. I care that you're a good person. That I can trust you."

"You can trust me. You can trust us," I reassure her. "Everything that happened was a stupid mistake born from my insecurities. I can't promise mistakes won't happen again. A relationship with three people, two of which are men, is bound to have mistakes, but I promise you can trust us, Riley. I swear it."

Jace kisses her hand. "I do too."

Riley casts a look between us. That familiar energy that we had on Christmas Eve sparks in the air, making it heavy and laced with need.

"You both want a relationship with me?" she asks timidly.

Jace and I grin stupidly at each other.

"If you'll have us," I say.

She lets out a sound of disbelief. "This is insane, you both know that? We all just met. You two have a history and I'm, I don't even know!"

Jace scoots over so he's practically plastered to Riley, then he brings one of his fingers up to tease her ear before he tugs on the lobe, causing her to shiver.

"We don't care if it's insane. We like you, Riley," he says in a husky voice.

"We more than like you," I add, my gaze burning into hers as I move even closer to her.

Riley rests her hand on my chest right over my heart. "It's not going to be easy," she whispers.

"I don't like easy," I say, putting my hand over hers. "Jace and I are hard workers. We go after what we want and we put in the time to do it. If you're not ready to be ours, Riley, then we'll wait. We'll do what it takes, but we want you in our lives. Whatever way you'll have us."

Jace kisses her shoulder and says, "We can go slow," the double meaning of his words turning up the heat in the room. Fuck, I think I'm starting to sweat.

Riley turns her face toward his so their lips are almost touching. My cock pushes against the placket of my jeans, and I lick my lips in anticipation as I watch them.

"And if I don't want to go slow?" she asks breathlessly.

A groan escapes my lips as Riley's hand starts to move down my chest toward my growing erection.

"We'll take you however you want to go, beautiful." Jace brushes his lips against hers, but before they can kiss, Riley pulls away, leaving him wanting.

"Under one condition," she says.

"Anything," Jace and I say together.

"No more lies. Even if they hurt. Even if we're scared. For this to work, we can't lie. Not about our feelings, what's going on in our lives. From this moment on, we tell the truth. It's not just my heart involved here, it's three."

I sit up a little straighter as her words settle in. She really is going to give us a chance. This beautiful, smart, unicorn of a woman is going to give us a chance. I feel like the luckiest asshole on the planet.

"No more lies," I say, my tone sure.

"No more lies," Jace agrees.

Riley surveys us quietly before the corners of her lips turn up. "No more lies," she echoes.

The promise of our words settles in like we've just signed a binding contract.

Then, I'm not sure who moves first. All at once we're a pile of limbs and hands as we come together. I feel Riley's lips on mine, then Jace's. There are hands on my cock then moving inside my sweater as Riley's shirt is thrown somewhere on the floor.

My mind tries to catch up to the feelings my body is experiencing, but I'm lost in soft moans, heated breaths, and warm skin. My cock leaks as Jace's rough hands work with Riley's delicate ones to tease and touch me in every place possible.

At some point we move to the bedroom, and there's no words, just sounds of pleasure as we explore and taste each other till my hard length is encased in Riley's heat like before and I can hear the snap of a lube cap as her breasts plaster to my chest. Jace inserts his cock and Riley cries in pleasure against my shoulder.

Then we're moving and kissing and making promises of what's to come and how nothing has ever felt so right before. I feel the ridges of Jace's cock moving against mine and he's whispering words of love in my ear that has me pulsing my come inside Riley's sex as she shatters and squeezes me with her own release, one so strong that it has Jace following right behind her.

I'm not sure how long the whole thing lasts, but as we cuddle together on a hotel bed in the honeymoon suite of a random hotel in downtown Seattle, I know one thing is for sure.

Santa did me a solid this Christmas.

Ho, ho, fucking, ho.

Epilogue

RILEY

One Year Later

SNOW FLUTTERS TO THE ground outside the penthouse window. It's late afternoon, and the sun is setting. Down below I can see the little dots of people milling about, out doing their Christmas Eve activities.

When my phone buzzes, my heart picks up speed. There's a message in our group chat that Leo named "Shortcake & Friends." Both Jace and I rolled our eyes at that, considering the three of us are far from "just friends," but it was kind of cute, so it stuck.

Leo: On our way home. ETA 15.
Jace: Hope that plug is keeping you company.

At the same time his message comes through, the plug starts buzzing. I let out a cry as I curse Jace and his toys with remotes. Since they both travel for work often, Jace upped his toy arsenal to include several with long-distance capabilities. The damn thing even works all the way from Europe. They claim it's their way of staying connected to me while away (in more ways than one). And when I tried to argue that's what FaceTime is for, I got the hottest spanking of my life with two of said toys inside me. My body flushes at the memory, and a flood of arousal pools between my legs.

Riley: I'd rather have your cocks to keep me company.
Leo : We know :)
Riley: Asshole.
Jace: Oooooh, that ass is gonna be red by the time we're done with it, beautiful.
Riley: Merry Christmas to me.

With a large grin, I put my phone away and head to the "man cave" which is now more of a "throuple cave." The best Christmas tree is there, along with where we keep our stockings and presents. It felt like the perfect place for the surprise I have planned. I know they're up to something, too. They were all secretive this morning saying they had to run out to grab a last-minute gift. I just waved them off and went to take a shower while they giggled like school boys and left.

My heart pounds in my chest as I think of them. My two men. It still feels surreal. It's been a year together. One whole year of kissing, cuddling, late night talks, tears, laughs and so much sex I'm surprised my vagina hasn't broken. I thought it would be difficult to exist in the world within a triad, and while that is true sometimes, for the most part, we've been lucky. Our families are accepting, though my dad was speechless for at least a month after we told him. I think it was more to do with Lucas McKnight's twin being one of my partners than anything else.

The media has been one of the biggest hurdles. They love to sneak blurry pictures of us and then try to pass them off as Lucas. Thankfully, that stopped working after a while, and it rarely happens now. Also, Lucas couldn't care less what people say about him and their speculations on if he shares his twin's sexuality or preferences. It put Leo at ease, especially after the pictures of us in the sports bar last year went viral. After that died down and we told our families, things just seem to work for us, despite normal couple fights and arguments. My phone buzzes, and I see Stevie's name.

Stevie: I know it's your anniversary and all, but why couldn't you celebrate here? Dad's got on A Christmas Story marathon and I want to shoot my own eye out.
Riley: Because then you'd all have to hear sex noises.
Stevie: Okay gross. But please tell me you'll be here tomorrow night like you promised. I need help. And booze. Jace always brings good booze. :)
Riley: We'll be there, with the good stuff.
Stevie: OK, fine. Enjoy your dicks. Speaking of dicks, congrats on finally ditching Chad. You deserve better than that agency and always have.

My body warms and I smile. Another thing to celebrate besides our anniversary is I'm finally celebrating kicking Chad and my "dream agency" to the curb. Starting in the New Year, I'm working at a new place on the Upper East Side. It's a smaller boutique agency that specializes in traditional advertising, but I was ready for a change. After my year with Jace and Leo, I realized something. My work wasn't making me happy anymore. I'm hoping this new change of pace will only lead to bigger and better things. Plus, I'll have more work from home hours, which will let me travel with the guys when I want.

I hear the sound of the front door opening and closing and quickly text Stevie.

Riley: Thanks, Sis. I'll see you tomorrow.
Stevie: Merry Dicking.

I bite my lip to keep from laughing, then turn off my phone. I smooth my hands down over my scantily-clad body and pull up my red and white striped socks before fluffing my curled hair. I spent the last few weeks acquiring the perfect "sexy candy cane" outfit to surprise the guys with, and I'm ready to be unwrapped.

"We're home, Shortcake!" Leo calls. "Where are you?"

The buzzing in my ass starts again, and I let out a squeak. Fucking Jace!

"She's in the cave," Jace says coyly.

The tune of "Santa Baby" plays softly over the speaker system and I close my eyes for a moment to let Eartha Kitt's sultry voice soothe my excited nerves. As I hear the boys' footsteps close in, I drop to my knees on the large tree skirt and put my eyes to the floor.

"Holy fucking shit," Leo says.

"Well, well, well." Jace hums. "So this is what our girl's been up to while we've been gone."

Arousal starts to coat my thighs, and the vibrations of the plug only add to my needy state.

"I guess someone wants to play." Leo chuckles. "I bet she's been dreaming of this all week. Haven't you, Candy Cane?"

I stifle a moan at the new nickname. "Yes, Sir."

Leo's purr of appreciation has me squeezing my thighs together.

Over the last year, we've explored a lot of things together. We've spent a considerable amount of time playing with dominance and submission. And while on any normal day we just fuck, make love, and have fun, we also enjoy switching around roles and seeing who likes what. I specifically chose to be submissive tonight as a reminder of last Christmas Eve.

"Eyes up," Leo commands.

I do as he says, my gaze connecting with two pairs of ravenous ones.

"Crawl to us," he adds, his voice steady.

My stomach flutters with butterflies as I move to my hands and knees. As I crawl, I make sure to keep my ass up, knowing that's how they both like it. When I reach their feet, I sit back on my knees as Jace leans down to grasp my jaw in his hand.

"You did this all for us, beautiful?"

"Yes, Daddy."

"Hmmm, you look sweet enough to eat. Doesn't she, baby?" He eyes Leo, who is already palming his hard cock through the front of his jeans.

"She does. But I think she gets that spanking first. I like my sweets soft and pliable."

Jace chuckles, his tone dark and husky. "You heard him, Riley. Now stand up, bend over the couch, and show us how wet that sweet pussy is."

I move as quickly as I can in the very tall red heels I chose, bending over the arm of the couch so my lace clad ass is in the air and my palms are pressing into the leather cushion.

"Good girl," Jace praises.

I can't see them from this position, but I hear them moving around. Their belt buckles jingle, and I take in the rustling of clothes and then the sounds of kissing. I can't help the groan that escapes. I love watching them kiss, and they know it. If they ever need to get me in the mood, one of them will grab the other and start going to town. The way they stroke each other's tongues and open up in such an intimate way—I can't get enough of it. After they torture me for a few more minutes, I finally sense a presence behind.

"Your ass is going to be as red as this pretty lace when we're done, Candy Cane," Leo says, pressing his hard cock into the seam of my ass. He exhales a breathy grunt as the fat head of his cock brushes over the buzzing plug while he dips one of his long fingers into my pussy.

"She's so wet already, J. Come and feel her."

Jace doesn't waste any time following Leo's request. I feel his massive cock brush against my heated skin as he steps closer, bringing his palms to rub the sensitive cheeks of my ass before moving down, down, down, until he's fingering me too. Wet sounds fill the room and all of us groan.

"Always ready for us. Always perfect," Jace says, moving so his lips are now near my ear, his beard tickling the sensitive skin there. "Just like the little slut you are."

As his degrading words wash over, he increases the vibrations in my ass, making my pussy clench around air. I can't stop the string of curses that follow.

"I think our little slut needs a gag, don't you?" Jace asks Leo thoughtfully.

"Stuff your cock down her throat, J. I want to see her choke on you while I turn her ass red."

I dig my fingertips into the cushions. My skin feels tight and itchy with need as I become hyper aware of the lace moving against my flushed skin, and how my hard nipples cut against the see-through bralette I'm wearing. I don't know why being spanked and used turns me on so much, but it's one of my favorite things. Maybe it's the ultimate trust that does it. And I've learned to trust them implicitly over the last year.

"With pleasure," Jace's voice cuts through my thoughts. "Open wide, beautiful."

I do as I'm told, opening my mouth to the point my jaw hurts so Jace can have his way with me. When the broad crown settles on my tongue, I hum around it, tasting the salty flavor of his leaking arousal. He starts slow at first, letting me get used to the weight and rhythm of his strokes. When I relax and start to take him deeper, Leo rubs his hands over my ass, pulling the lace down so it's around my knees.

"I love these stockings," he admires. "I want to fuck you in only these at some point tonight while Jace eats you alive." Leo pauses for a moment, letting the anticipation build, then says, "Now don't bite Jace's dick off, Shortcake."

Jace grunts just as Leo's hand comes down on my left ass cheek. Then my right. I cry out around Jace's thickness as the slaps begin raining down in various degrees of strength. Leo is the master of spanking. He knows just how much I can take, the kind of pressure I like, and when to pull back and then keep going.

Jace pushes my hair from my face. "You're so beautiful like this, taking my cock, letting Leo do whatever he wants to you. You're perfect for us, Riley. Just perfect."

Tears start to fill my eyes as the slaps get stronger and Jace's dick goes deeper. When he hits the back of my throat I hold off my gag, enjoying his praise when I do. This goes on for a while, Jace fucking my throat and Leo turning my ass his favorite color. I start to fade into a sex high, all the endorphins and serotonin flooding my desperate body.

When the slaps suddenly stop and Jace's cock leaves my mouth, I miss the attention for only two seconds before Leo's tongue laps at my folds. I let out a garbled noise of pleasure, my fingers trying to grip the leather couch but failing.

"Does that feel good, slut?" Jace asks, running a hand through my hair.

"Yes!"

"Yes what?"

"Yes, Daddy!"

Jace growls his approval. "Since you've been such a good girl, Leo's going to let you come. Then you're going to take his cock so deep you'll feel him for a week. And you know what I'm going to be doing?" I shake my head. "Fucking Leo so hard into that pussy that you'll both beg for mercy."

"God yes," I moan. "Please, please, please. I want that so bad."

"I love it when you beg," Jace says, bending over to kiss me sloppily, the kind of open-mouthed kiss that leaves no room for breath or thought.

I mumble out another slew of random words as Leo flicks my clit and fingers me deep. It doesn't take much for him to make me come, my arousal coating my thighs and body clenching around his long digits as I float off into bliss.

The next thing I know, I'm being moved around like I weigh nothing. Jace settles me back against the chaise lounge stacked with pillows, ripping the remaining lace from my body but leaving the candy cane stockings on for Leo.

When Leo's icy eyes come into view, his mouth glistening with my come, I'm once again stunned by his beauty. Not only that, but how lucky I am to have him in my life. He wastes no time and gets on the chaise between my legs, looping his hands under my thighs so my legs are up and spread wide, getting me into the position he needs to enter me. He keeps one of his legs bent over the edge of the lounge with his foot planted so he can get momentum and so Jace can enter him.

"Ready to get fucked, Shortcake?" he chirps, his one-dimple indenting his flushed cheek.

"Are you, Beefcake?" I tease.

He expels a bawdy laugh just before he pinches my thigh. I squeal and squirm.

"Still a brat, I see."

"Always, Sir."

Leo releases a groan. "You're going to be the death of me, Riley."

The feeling is mutual.

The sound of Jace opening a bottle of lube has us coming out of our little bubble. After a short kiss, Leo moves to position his cock at my entrance. He gives his length a few languid strokes, watching my reaction as he dips the head in and out of my heat. The plug is still buzzing softly in my ass, but I've gotten used to it enough that it adds a nice fullness. It will also make Leo lose his mind when he feels it, which is why Jace leaves it inside me.

"I like you stuffed, baby," is what he always likes to say.

As Leo sinks in, inch by glorious inch, my head falls back against the pillows.

"Fuck, Shortcake. You feel so warm, so tight," he keens, his lips seeking mine as he bottoms out. "I love when you have the plug inside you. Goddamn, it's so fucking good."

"Leo!" I cry, gripping his arms as I adjust to his size. A size I've both gotten used to and also one that I never will.

"Hmm, I love watching you fuck our girl, baby." Jace groans, his hands tracing the muscles and divots of Leo's back. Once he's done appreciating his form, he squirts a very generous amount of lube on his cock and between Leo's ass cheeks. Moaning, Leo seeks out my lips again as Jace gets into position, rimming Leo with his fingers, getting him ready for his massive cock.

Jace soothes him with sweet words that have my clit throbbing and my orgasm drawing nearer. Leo curses and drops his head to my shoulder as Jace starts to push into Leo's body. The action thrusts Leo's cock impossibly deeper inside me—to the point I can feel it in my womb. It feels sinful, a little painful, but also euphoric. My arousal only strengthens when I take in the faces of the two men I love.

"Oh fuck, oh fuck. Feels so fucking good, J!" Leo grunts. I choose that moment to squeeze my pussy around him and he tenses, crying out again.

"Your ass is perfect, baby. So fucking tight," Jace says, slapping Leo's tight end for good measure. Leo releases a muffled noise against the crook of my neck as Jace feeds himself in, his balls slapping against Leo's sensitive skin when he's all the way inside him. I can't help the whine that tumbles out of me from the force of it.

"You're both so big! It feels like you're fucking me too, Jace!" I cry.

He groans out a sound of approval as he starts to move, placing his hands on the back of Leo's shoulders to gain more power. We do this position so often that it takes no time for them to find a good rhythm. As Leo thrusts into me harder, Jace does the same, forcing Leo deeper and deeper inside my pussy. I never really understood the "dicked down" phrase until I started sleeping with them. I swear sometimes I can feel them all the way to my throat.

I close my eyes for a moment to enjoy all the sensations. Between Leo's cock, his lips, the plug and Jace's deep punishing thrusts, I'm close to coming again. I dig my nails into Leo's hair as he plants open-mouthed kisses down my collar bone. When I open my eyes, I find his brow pinched and there's a sheen of sweat on his forehead, a telltale sign he's about to come.

"Are you close, beautiful?" Jace asks me.

I nod, tightening my inner walls around Leo so he's cursing.

"Fuck her harder, Leo. Make her come," Jace demands of him in that oh-so-sexy daddy voice.

Leo does as he's told, his hips punching forward in shallow thrusts so I'm crying out and thanking every deity I can think of. Jace grabs Leo's hips and matches the brutal pace, pounding over and over again so I can hear the smacking of their skin and my breasts bounce heavily from the momentum. The added movement only adds to my impending release.

"Fuck me harder," Leo begs, one of his hands reaching back to grip Jace's tattooed thigh.

He acquiesces, grunting and swearing till his shoulders tense and I know he's going to come any second. Leo gently bites the skin of neck and that finally does me in.

"I'm coming!" I scream, clinging to my men as the earth shatters around me and my body convulses with pleasure.

"Fuck, I'm coming, too. Come with me, Jace," Leo shouts, his movements turning erratic as he gets closer to his release. I pry my eyes open to watch as Jace pistons his hips, slapping the cheeks of Leo's ass. They both let out sounds of pleasure at the contact.

When Jace locks eyes with me, I mouth "I love you," and it sends him over the edge. With a final thrust, he growls out his release, giving Leo his orgasm alongside him. They both pant heavily, their sounds of pleasure music to my ears as I float in my post-orgasm high.

A short time later, as we cuddle under the Christmas tree, our skin sticky with come and sweat, I can't help but think how I ended up here.

"Penny for your thoughts," Leo asks me, lifting his head from Jace's chest.

I stare into his eyes, my heart squeezing at the love I see there. "Just thinking how smart I was for going home with a stranger last Christmas."

Leo's smile grows wider. "I'm glad, too. Speaking of…we have an anniversary present for you, Shortcake." He looks at Jace and he nods, like he's giving him the go-ahead for something.

Before I can ask what it is, Leo's standing up in all his naked glory, searching for his pants that were discarded on the floor earlier. As I wait, Jace pulls me closer into his warmth, kissing my forehead and stroking my back. It takes only a couple seconds for Leo to pull a small red pouch out of his pants pocket. He returns to his spot next to Jace and hands it to me, his fingers brushing mine as he does.

"Open it, baby," Jace encourages. I take the bag and untie the red ribbon. When I open it, I see a red box at the bottom. Goosebumps break out over my skin as I realize it's a ring box. I think I stop breathing as I pull it out.

"Is this where you went this morning?" I ask.

Jace and Leo chuckle.

"It is. Now open it!" Leo says, giddy like a child on Christmas morning. So unlike the Scrooge I met a year ago.

I take the delicate red box and turn it so the latch is facing me, their eyes observing me carefully as I open it. What I reveal inside has me gasping for breath. There are three platinum rings tucked inside, two are obviously large enough to fit their fingers, and one has three small diamonds on it. My eyes start to water as I look up at the two men I love more than anything in this world.

"We know we can't legally marry each other," Leo says softly. "But we want you to be ours, Riley. In every way we can possibly think of."

Jace tucks a lock of hair behind my ear, his smile adoring. "What Leo means to ask is, will you marry us, Riley?"

My eyes dart between them, their smiles bright. In most cases, a woman would probably want to be proposed to with clothes on, or maybe after a nice meal or some elaborate proposal, but this? Us together, naked under an overly decorated Fraser fir on Christmas Eve? It fits us perfectly.

I let out a sob, practically tackling them as I hug them tightly.

"Is that a yes?" Leo laughs.

"It's a yes!" I cry.

Then we're kissing and sobbing and Leo is sliding the ring on my finger. The tears really start to flow as Jace and Leo put the rings they've picked out on each other's fingers. It's a tender moment, one I wish I filmed. The love between them is strong and unwavering. It makes my entire body sing.

After the excitement has calmed a bit, we stare at our joined hands with matching rings in a warm silence.

"Now we need some turtle doves and a partridge in a pear tree," Leo jokes.

Jace chuckles, the ring on his finger. "That's not how the song goes, baby. It's five golden rings."

"Five is way too many. It should be three," he argues.

I shrug. "I don't know, five could be fun."

Jace and Leo go quiet, their heads whipping to stare at me.

After a moment, I let out a snort. "Kidding!"

Jace smirks. "As I've said before, our girl's got jokes."

Or do I?

Acknowledgements

WOW! HERE WE ARE. At the end of my fifth published book. I can't believe it!

I'll make these acknowledgements quick and dirty...just like this novella.

First and foremost, I have to say thank you to YOU, my reader. Without you, I wouldn't be getting to share my stories with so many people. Thank you for being a champion of my books. For being a champion of diverse and plus-size characters. Every time you read and share my books, you show the world that these stories matter. That love for ALL matters. So thank you. Thank you, thank you, THANK YOU!

I also need to give massive love and a big shout out to Melissa (IG: @melrosereadsromance) and Melissa (IG: @looksandbooks2022) for being my sounding boards for this story. You really helped me make Trick Shot what it is. I can't thank you enough for your love and support and for reading my midnight texts and listening to my long voice notes. I love you both so much.

Thank you to my forever Ride or Die, Nic (IG: @nic_reeves_writes). Meeting you in 2019 has been such a blessing. Thank you for encouraging me, even when you think my ideas are nuts. You make me a better writer, and I'm so blessed to have you as a friend.

I'd also like to say a big thank you to my beta and sensitivity readers: Noelle, Bree, Bella, Brittany, Brandy, Melissa, and Melissa! Thank you for reading Trick Shot and making it better.

And I can't forget, of course, my editor: Swati Hegde! Working with you is such a dream. Thank you for making me a better writer and fixing all my dangling modifiers and commas. You're the best!

And since I'm true to my word, I also have to thank my writer and fellow author friend M.A. Wardell. Thanks for teaching me about the importance of rimming. Jace and Leo thank you, too! (I told you I'd thank you in my book!)

Lastly, I need to thank and acknowledge my late friend Sally.

Sally, you may not be on this earth with us, but I felt you every step of the way while I was writing Trick Shot. I know you would have LOVED this book, you dirty dog! I miss you so much.

Thanks again to everyone who has loved and supported me through the difficult and wonderful process of writing another book. I hope you enjoyed it.

Merry Christmas & Happy Holidays!

Xoxo,

Kayla

Want More Leo, Riley, and Jace?

Get Their Bonus Chapter at www.patreon.com/kaylagrosse

More Books by Kayla Grosse

PUCK SHY (BROTHER PUCKERS BOOK #2)
a spicy novella with a plus-size female lead and her golden
retriever hockey player

SILVER FOXED
a dad's best friend, spicy age gap novella with a plus-size female
lead and her sexy silver fox

REIN ME IN (THE COWBOYS OF NIGHT HAWK #1)
a late brother's best friend, small town, cowboy romance with a
plus-size cowgirl

ROPE ME IN (THE COWBOYS OF NIGHT HAWK #2)
a small town, country boy meets city girl romance with a
plus-size female lead

I LIKE YOU LIKE THAT
a second chance, rock star romance with a plus-size female lead

AXES AND O'S
Available November 4th, 2024
a super spicy MMF snowed-in lumbersnack romance

FALLING FOR THE MANNY
a single mom, contemporary romance by author duo Kayla
Nicole

For Exclusive Bonus Stories, Artwork, and More Visit:
www.patreon.com/kaylagrosse

Find Kayla:

Website: www.kaylagrosse.com
Instagram: @kaylawriteslife
Facebook: Kaylaholics Facebook Group
TikTok: @kaylagrossewriter
Twitter: @kaylagrosse

Printed in Great Britain
by Amazon

44878252R00111